DEVILS IN THE DARK
TERROR TRIOS
FEATURING HUGH B. CAVE

DEVILS IN THE DARK
TERROR TRIOS
FEATURING HUGH B. CAVE

INTRODUCTION BY
John Pelan

BOSTON
ALTUS PRESS
2012

© 2012 Altus Press • First Edition—2012

EDITED AND DESIGNED BY
Matthew Moring

PUBLISHING HISTORY

"Three Caves of Terror" appears here for the first time. Copyright © 2012 John Pelan. All Rights Reserved.

"Devils in the Dark" originally appeared in the February, 1934 issue of *Dime Mystery Magazine*. Copyright © 2012 Argosy Communications, Inc. All Rights Reserved. Reprinted by arrangement with Argosy Communications, Inc.

"Inn of the Shadow-Creatures" originally appeared in the December, 1934 issue of *Dime Mystery Magazine*. Copyright © 1934 by Popular Publications, Inc. Copyright renewed © 1961 and assigned to Argosy Communications, Inc. All Rights Reserved.

"Dark Bondage" originally appeared in the January, 1935 issue of *Dime Mystery Magazine*. Copyright © 1935 by Popular Publications, Inc. Copyright renewed © 1962 and assigned to Argosy Communications, Inc. All Rights Reserved.

Published by arrangement with Argosy Communications, Inc.

THANKS TO
Joel Frieman, Rick Ollerman, John Pelan & David White

ALL RIGHTS RESERVED

No part of this book may be reproduced or utilized in any form or by any means, electronic or mechanical, without permission in writing from the publisher.

This edition has been marked via subtle changes, so anyone who reprints from this collection is committing a violation of copyright.

Visit altuspress.com for more books like this.

Printed in the United States of America.

TABLE OF CONTENTS

THREE CAVES OF TERROR *by John Pelan* I

DEVILS IN THE DARK I

INN OF THE SHADOW-CREATURES 55

DARK BONDAGE 115

HUGH B. CAVE

THREE CAVES OF TERROR

USUALLY THESE introductions serve to introduce an obscure master of the macabre to a new generation of readers. However, it's hard to imagine any fan of weird fiction being unfamiliar with Hugh B. Cave.... After all, in a career that spanned seventy years of active writing, Cave (unlike many of his contemporaries) never really left the field for any extended period of time. Even during the down times for the horror genre, Cave would still turn out the occasional story. There are also the hundreds of stories in other genres, adventure, mystery, and mainstream tales appearing in some of the most prestigious slicks.

Here we're concerned strictly with his career in horror fiction, the weird menace genre in particular.... Cave began with a couple of contributions to *Ghost Stories* and quickly moved to *Weird Tales* and *Strange Tales* in 1932. When *Dime Mystery Magazine* changed its format from reprinting dull mystery novels to the new genre invented by editor Rogers Terrill, Cave was featured in the seminal October, 1933 issue making him one of the first authors of the genre that would come to be known as "weird menace."

During the next few years Hugh Cave was a million words a year man with a prodigious output covering all genres but he always retained a fondness for the rationalized supernatural tale featured so prominently in *Dime Mystery Magazine, Terror Tales* and *Horror Stories*. The basic weird menace story was formulaic in nature; the essential elements were a seemingly supernatural menace wreaking havoc. The heroine would generally be captured by the vampire/ghoul/werewolf/what-have-you and in most cases would lose most of her clothing in the process of being tortured. The denouement of the tale would reveal a human agency behind the seemingly supernatural occurrences and the goal of these activities usually revolved around gaining control of an inheritance, valuable land, or hidden wealth of some sort. In short, the plots strongly resembled an episode of *Scooby-Doo* with the main difference being that Velma and Daphne were never stripped naked and tortured (at least, not that I recall…).

Despite such a strict formula, a creative author such as Hugh Cave could find myriad ways to put his own spin on things. Along with Arthur Leo Zagat, Cave specialized in what the editors optimistically called "book length novels." In actuality, these were pieces of fifteen thousand to twenty-five thousand words in length; a length that as a horror writer myself, I find to be the perfect vehicle to sustain a sense of mounting dread, develop three-dimensional characters, and include a twist or two without having to resort to padding with unnecessary sub-plots or expository dialogue.

An examination of Cave's bibliography shows that when it came to the weird menace magazines the vast majority of his contributions were in excess of ten thousand words. The only downside to working at this length is that anthologists can rarely use more than one or two such pieces per book and many editors shied away from such lengthy works entirely. When Matt Moring and I developed the concept of the "Terror Trios" series it was with the idea that Hugh B. Cave would be our "flagship author" and the series would be built around his many novellas.

While most of Cave's contemporaries are long since forgotten, Cave remained more or less in the limelight throughout the 1950s-1970s due in a large part to a handful of genre novels and a willingness to correspond with fans both in the U.S. and the U.K. While many of his contemporaries such as Blassingame and Knox has faded from the public eye, Cave remained visible if not downright prominent via reprints in Robert W. Lowndes' digest publications, *The Magazine of Horror* and *Startling Mystery*.

In the 1970s Stuart David Schiff started *Whispers* as a thematic continuance of *Weird Tales* magazine. Schiff immediately tabbed Cave as a contributor to his publication, with Cave's first appearance coming in 1974 with "Take Me, for Instance." This appeared in the November, 1974 issue, and was followed up with additional stories in *Whispers* and more importantly, a massive collection from Carcosa Press, *Murgunstrumm and Other Stories*, as well as the followup volumes *Death Stalks the Night* and *The Door Below* from Fedogan & Bremer. Finally, when Stephen Jones revived the classic *Not at Night* series, Cave appeared in each volume. Active for over seventy years, Hugh B. Cave enjoyed one of the longest careers in horror fiction and this collection of novellas will give the reader a chance to see where it all began....

John Pelan
Midnight House
Gallup, NM

HUGH B. CAVE

DEVILS IN THE DARK

Why did the killer, sating his blood-lust in the dark, prey only upon those nearest and dearest to Matthew Haley? Who would next keep a ghastly midnight rendezvous with the black-clad intruder—whose evil gift was sudden, agonizing death?

MR. *MORGAN BELZAK*, senior partner of the Belzak-Haley Department Stores, Inc., paced slowly down the first-floor corridor of the Peterboro Apartments, produced a ring of keys from a pocket of his oxford-gray overcoat and let himself into apartment number seven. Extending a plump hand to the light-switch near the door, he thumbed it awkwardly, then closed the door behind him and paraded into the expensively furnished living room.

A clock on the living room mantel said three A.M., and Morgan Belzak hiccoughed noisily as he peered at it. The lateness of the hour did not trouble him. Yesterday the auditors had checked the books of the Belzak-Haley Company, and the figures had revealed a profit for the first time in three years. Morgan Belzak had determined to celebrate the occasion. He had done so. Now he was quite drunk.

With middle-aged sluggishness he removed his coat and hat and placed them on the somber-hued divan at one end of the room. His suit-coat and necktie he draped over the back of a chair before scuffing into the kitchen and pouring himself a drink.

Glass in hand, he returned to the living room and sat at the antique mahogany desk in the corner.

He sat there a long while before remembering his reason for doing so. Then he finished his drink, made a face over the empty glass, and pawed open the center drawer of the desk. His companion for the best part of the evening had been a charming young lady who had begun by being a stranger and ended by being something far more entertaining. He had promised to send her a check.

Laboriously he unscrewed the cap of his fountain pen, opened the checkbook, and looked at the desk calendar in front of him to make sure of the date. He did not hear the almost inaudible tread of naked feet behind him. He did not turn to see the hunch-shouldered, black-cloaked figure which moved softly toward him from the doorway leading to the dining room.

Boring eyes studied the back of Morgan Belzak's stooped head. Gaunt hands rose slowly upward to the level of the unsuspecting man's neck. Had Belzak turned, had he looked into the contorted face of the cloaked menace behind him, he might have stumbled erect in time to escape. But he did not turn. He was concerned only with the checkbook in front of him, and with the failure of his fountain pen to operate properly.

The cloaked figure came to a stop directly behind him and stood there, glaring down hungrily. Hooked fingers hung above Belzak's neck, then shot forward with uncanny quickness and fastened in soft flesh. The doomed man had no chance. He stiffened, and a single short grunt escaped his throat; then he was dragged backward and hurled to the floor. And the cloaked figure fell upon him.

Morgan Belzak looked up into the face of his assailant, and screamed. His wide open eyes saw white, tight-drawn skin, carmine lips and sunken cheeks. Frantically he tore at the murderous hands which encircled his throat. Madly he strove to free himself from the weight of his assailant's body. Then the hooked fingers fastened deeper in his neck; the white face descended triumphantly with gaping mouth. Cruel teeth sank into him. His lurid scream became a gurgle, and ended in silence.

The clock on the mantel ticked on, its big hand moving sluggishly across five spaces, then five more—and five more.

Finally the cloaked figure stood erect, gazing down at Morgan Belzak's dead body. A soft, triumphant laugh echoed in the silent room. Slowly, unemotionally the intruder turned and paced to the door through which Belzak had entered the apartment twenty minutes before.

The door opened, closed silently. On the mantel, the clock ticked on relentlessly. Morgan Belzak lay alone in death, his throat ripped open, his eyes fixed wide with horror—his body drained of blood.

CHAPTER TWO

BEYOND RETURN

A COLD, RAW wind swept across the Brookline Reservoir and clawed angrily at Stephen Wayne's bent body as he paced uphill along the half-cleared sidewalk of Verne Street. New England, in January, could be vicious, despite the hypocritical ballyhoo of native New Englanders who kept one eye shut and wore a rose-colored glass over the other. Here in Chestnut Hill, amid expensive homes of upper-crust Bostonians January could be an excellent advertisement to lure normal young men to healthier climes. The fact that many of the expensive homes were closed and shuttered, abandoned for the winter, was proof of that!

Stephen Wayne, trudging along Verne Street with both hands wedged deep in the pockets of his raglan overcoat, hat-brim pulled down to shield his frowning features, thought grimly of southern resorts and wondered if the loveliness and charm of twenty-two year old Gloria Haley were really of sufficient weight to balance the discomforts of Boston's unruly climate. He, Stephen Wayne, was in Boston because Gloria Haley had begged him to remain—and because the sight of the murdered, mutilated body of Morgan Belzak, erstwhile partner and business associate of Gloria Haley's church-loving, widowed father, had aroused the bloodhound instincts which had lain dormant in Steve Wayne ever since he had deserted police headquarters and become a private "investigator" who seldom allowed business to interfere with pleasure.

"I'm afraid!" Gloria had said, putting out a trembling hand to cling to Steve's arm. "I'm afraid, Steve! Why should anyone want to kill Belzak that way? If it was for business reasons, then my father may be in danger, too. You've got to help me, Steve!"

No man could have refused; least of all Steve Wayne, who, despite his mania for running around the country—or perhaps because of that mania—was amazingly susceptible to feminine allure. Moreover he knew the Haleys well, had known them for years, had even on several occasions asked Gloria Haley to say something more than: "Well, maybe someday, Steve." So now, at nine A.M., an unearthly hour for Steve Wayne to be up and abroad, he was parading down Verne Street toward the big brown house on the corner of Porter.

He scowled again when he looked up at the mansion-like structure. Strangely enough, the front path had not been cleared of snow, and was beaten solid by the imprint of many feet. The door hung open. Loose snow had drifted across the threshold into the hallway.

He climbed the steps slowly, put a finger on the bell, and walked in. Voices were audible from the far end of the corridor. He strode forward, wondering why Mannix, the butler, had not made a hurried appearance at the bell's shrill clamor.

Mannix did make an appearance then. He was a short fat man, attired in gloomy black which accentuated the smoothness of his pate, and he came jerkily from the library, blinking his eyes and rubbing his hands together as if to warm them.

He said: "Oh, it's you Mr. Wayne!" and seemed more at ease. Something had happened to disturb his usually undisturbable attitude of slow-footed efficiency. He even looked afraid.

Steve peered at him critically and said, "Where's Miss Haley?"

"She's in the librar—" The butler checked himself. "If you'll wait in the back study, sir, I'll tell her you're here."

Steve nodded, shot a sharp glance at the man and walked down the dark, drafty corridor. He knew the Haley house well. Built in the late 'eighties by Haley's father, the present owner had left it untouched, excepting for the substitution of electricity for gaslight. Rambling, and dismal, it was furnished with the elaborate gimcrackery of a bygone age. Empty, armored figures loomed from the dark corners of the hall; massive furniture, like huge, sleeping animals crouched in the gloomy interior.

Steve Wayne noticed that the folding double doors of the library were closed and as he passed, curious, he caught the glint of the metal lock in the crack between the doors. From within came the sound of hushed voices. Although the words were indistinguishable, Steve Wayne stopped, ears alert, nerves tingling.

There was no mistaking it—stark fear and horror came to him in the tense tones of those lowered voices.

JAW set, Steve stepped forward. He knew that the library opened into the next room beyond, and he was just turning into it when a heavy hand grasped his shoulder. He whirled to see Mannix's fat, sweat-beaded face close to his own.

"My God, Mister Wayne, don't—" And the man seemed to recover himself. "Pardon me, sir. Mr. Haley's strict orders are that no one is to go inside the library." His voice was desperate, pleading. "Please, sir, the back study—"

Gray, steel-like eyes bored into the butler's fear-filled pupils. "Okay, Mannix. But what the hell—?"

The distant echo of a bell-pull sounded. Mannix wet his lips. "Yes, sir. The back study—" and was off to answer the summons.

Steve swore under his breath, hesitated, and then with a shrug of his broad shoulders entered the gloomy room to which he had been directed.

A dim yellow bulb seemed to accentuate the gloom more than to dispell it. The place was packed with a weird assortment of furniture. A priceless Adam highboy was jammed against a huge ruffled davenport; mission oak mingled with Sheraton pieces, and velvet drapes with fringed lambrequins seemed to hang from every conceivable corner. Shadows, and a musty, airless smell….

Steve shook himself, as if to ward off an evil spell wrought by the gloom. Although it was warm enough there, he felt an uncomfortable chill race down his spine.

He got up from his chair and moved toward the curtained aperture which should, he knew, open onto the room adjoining the library. And then, his hand on the door-knob, he paused. Footsteps sounded beyond the closed door. Two pairs of feet, advancing slowly into that adjoining room.

From beyond the closed door Matthew Haley's gruff voice raised suddenly in anger.

"You can't have her, Ebbarton—you hear me? You can't have her now. You—you're too late."

There came the creak of a chair, and another voice spoke evenly.

"Did it ever occur to you, Matthew, that I might be able to give the police some interesting information about your ancestors—information which might have direct bearing on the death of Morgan Belzak?"

Steve Wayne, listening beyond the door, stiffened. He could imagine Matthew Haley's gaunt eyes flashing fire.

There was a moment of silence—silence that hung freighted with tension. Then, in a perfectly expressionless tone, Haley said, "You've let self-sympathy unbalance your mind, Ebbarton. You—you abused Julia when she was your wife. Do you think any such foolish charge against me would bring her back to you now?"

The chair creaked again, and the man addressed as Ebbarton spoke pleadingly. "I'm giving you this chance, Haley, merely because, like a damned fool, I'm sentimental. We were friends once—good ones! Until you literally stole my wife. She—got a divorce, of course. And now you're—going to marry her!" His voice was bitter, somehow pittiable.

Suddenly then he cried out harshly, "Well—I want her back! You understand? The past two years I've lost everything—my wife—all my money. Damn the money. But Julia—damn it, Haley. I need her! I'm not young any more—"

His voice was thick, emotion-choked.

Matthew Haley laughed, and his words were measured, mingling loathing and contempt. "You—miserable—blackmailer!" he said.

Ebbarton's voice, when he answered, was increasingly hysterical. "She loves me, damn you! *Me*—understand! You—you've done something to her—changed her in some frightful way—"

"She came to me of her own accord, as you well know," Haley said calmly. "Came because she couldn't stand your torturing her. My God! You should know. I saw the unhealed scars on her arms, on her neck—"

"I have a beastly temper. She's high-strung as hell—so'm I. But I swear to you! Oh, for God's sake, send her back to me, Matthew!"

Matthew Haley said nothing.

"All right. All right! I gave you your chance." Steve Wayne heard Ebbarton getting up from his chair, moving across the floor toward the hall door. "My attorneys will notify you the first thing Monday morning, Matthew. I'm starting suit against you for alienation."

"Alienation of affections? On account of—Julia?" Matthew Haley's voice was dangerously soft.

"Yes. For one hundred thousand dollars. And—and, by God! when I get it, I'll take the check and turn it over to any charity you name—badly as I need the money. 'Blackmail,' you said! Ahh!"

Haley's voice, when he spoke again, seemed that of an old, broken man.

"John," he said, "that—that suit would be quite useless. I no longer have Julia's affections. She—she's left me!"

Ebbarton grunted. "Left you?" he echoed. "Good God! Where—when—"

Matthew Haley spoke slowly. "Julia," he said, "was murdered sometime last night. It is ghastly—horrible— Her throat—" He stopped, controlled himself. "She met her death, John, in the identical manner that Morgan Belzak met his. Come into the library."

SWEAT stood out on Steve Wayne's brow as the footfalls of the two men diminished. He stood up slowly, grasping the back of a chair. Julia Ebbarton the second victim! Who would be next? What was this horrible fate that wreaked its terrifying, bloody murder upon those who stood close to Matthew Haley?

Quick, light footfalls sounded outside the hall door. Swiftly Steve crossed to it, unlocked it. Gloria, strikingly beautiful in crimson and black lounging pajamas stood there. He could see that she was suffering under a strain; lack of sleep had made her eyes unusually bright; lines of nervousness were about her mouth.

But her chin was up.

She smiled. "Mannix said you were waiting. Sorry, Steve, I couldn't get away— Then she stopped, reading something intuitively in Steve's face. "You—you've heard it?" she shuddered. "Ugh—it's like a nightmare! And—damn it—I'm afraid, Steve. Afraid for father!"

He put a reassuring hand upon her arm. His voice was clipped. "You—and he are all right, Gloria. I'm going into the library. Don't come unless you want to."

But she walked with him, her eyes wide, her face pale. "Thank God you've come, Steve!" she whispered.

The inner library door was open. Steve stood on the threshold, staring. Inside the richly furnished room half a dozen people were assembled. Matthew Haley and another man his own age—evidently Ebbarton—were there, bent over something that lay on the divan. Two uniformed policemen stood awkwardly by a heavy, walnut table. A servant girl was gaping at Inspector Frank Moody of Headquarters, who was parading importantly up and down the luxurious Persian rug. For a moment no one was aware of Steve's presence.

He paced forward and stared at the thing on the divan. His own eyes widened, and he stood rigid a moment before advancing to Matthew Haley's side. Then he gazed down in horror at the woman's half-naked body, shuddering involuntarily.

The rather attractive divorced wife of John Ebbarton lay there, her sightless eyes staring at the ceiling. Her plump body was torn, hideously mangled. Her face was a mask of utter terror; her eyes dilated, her mouth frozen open. Her throat was ripped horribly, just as the throat of Morgan Belzak had been ripped.

Slowly John Ebbarton rose to his feet, walked to the door of the room. Then the front door closed with a muffled thud.

STEVE made fists of his hands, shoved them solidly against his hips, and stood staring. His mind played with the problem, sorting out those elements which seemed important, and holding them up for mental examination. Here was a mystery horrible enough to make even Steve Wayne shudder, and Steve, despite the fact that his years of life numbered only twenty-six, was not unfamiliar with murder in its most gruesome forms. His hankering for things unusual and dangerous had taken him into more than one strange maze.

He looked at Inspector Moody, and Moody said nothing. Moody was no halfwit, either. He had a brain, knew how to use it. But this business evidently had him stumped. As for the others, the two cops were still minding their own business, Matthew Haley was standing motionless by the divan, the servant girl was still gaping goggle-eyed, and Gloria was looking expectantly at Steve.

"When did it happen?" Steve demanded.

Haley made a choking sound in his throat and mumbled thickly: "Last night—sometime. I—I found her this morning when I went to call her for breakfast. She was my guest, and—"

And she was the woman Haley loved. That was important. Morgan Belzak had been Haley's partner, and this woman would soon have been Haley's wife. Someone, some inhuman fiend who fed on horror, had deliberately wiped out the two persons who occupied first and second place in Haley's esteem. First and second? Well, maybe. There was Gloria. Steve glanced at her and felt suddenly afraid for her. She was Haley's daughter. Unless he was guessing wrong, she was in horrible danger.

He strode to her side and drew her toward the door. She let him lead her into the corridor; then she leaned against the wall and stared at him helplessly.

"What can we do, Steve?"

"Tell me what you know."

"I—I don't know anything. Mrs. Ebbarton was staying here for the weekend. This morning father went to her room to call her for breakfast, and—and I heard him scream. I ran upstairs and found him kneeling beside her. She was dead, Steve. Then I called the police. Father didn't want me to, but I did it anyway. And Inspector Moody came, with the policemen, and they carried the body downstairs, and—that's all."

Steve nodded, and looked up sharply as the servant girl appeared in the doorway. The girl was a blonde, with saucer eyes and a scared, thin face. She came forward timidly. She had worked for the Haleys' more than a year now. Her name was Olga something, and she was supposed to be Hungarian. Haley had a yen for foreigners.

The girl licked her lips and said: "Please, sir, can I speak with you alone? It's about—about the thing that killed Mrs. Ebbarton."

Steve glanced at Gloria. Gloria frowned and said: "She has some foolish idea. She tried to tell it to Inspector Moody, and he wouldn't listen."

The servant girl put a hand on Steve's arm. Steve shrugged, drew her aside, waited for her to speak. She licked her lips again and began to talk jerkily, hoarsely:

"Yes, sir, I did try to tell Inspector Moody, and I know what I'm talking about! It isn't long since I came to this country, and I haven't forgot all I knew before I came here. Maybe you don't believe in vampires, but I do. I've lived where they are, and people are feared of them. And it was a vampire that killed Mrs. Ebbarton! No one else would have drunk all the blood out of her body like that!"

The girl's eyes were full of genuine terror. Steve looked into them and saw something else—saw the mental images behind the terror. Maybe she was right; maybe Belzak and the Ebbarton woman had been murdered by the kind of monster she had in mind. Not the legendary type of vampire, not the blood-eating, dead-alive vampire who crawled from its grave at sunset and feasted on death during the hours of darkness, but a human fiend with vampirical tendencies. Stranger things were written in the big red book, and they were not superstitious claptrap either, but cold fact.

Steve said: "All right, sister. Thanks."

He strode back into the library and found Gloria waiting for him. She took his hand, looked into his face.

"You'll stay here, Steve? You won't leave me?"

"You're right I'll stay," he scowled.

He meant it, even though Matthew Haley was staring at him queerly and coming forward to talk to him. Matthew Haley, religious and methodical in his mode of living, had always frowned upon Steve's life-is-what-you-make-it-and-to-hell-with-the-consequences attitude. Haley and Steve Wayne were not the best of friends.

CHAPTER THREE

The Clock Ticks On

*A*FTER THE simple funeral ceremony, held in the Haley house the following day, Steve and Gloria accompanied Matthew Haley to the cemetery. A cheerless cold sleet was blowing up from Boston Harbor as they drove through the ornate iron gateway.

Red-eyed from lack of sleep, following his night's vigil in the house, Steve stood with the little group as the minister read the last words over the remains of Julia Ebbarton. For a moment they bowed their heads and Steve, glancing toward Matthew Haley, noted how he had aged in that one night. And suddenly, he was aware of a strange sound behind him—a snuffled sob—and yet not quite that.

He turned, to see the peculiarly thin face of John Ebbarton, now twisted in grief. Ebbarton seemed to move as a man in a dream. He came close to Matthew Haley, standing at one side of Steve. Even though Steve moved away, guiding Gloria back toward the car, he heard the disconnected words from Ebbarton's lips.

"Sorry—must have been crazy yesterday, Matthew.... It's hell, I guess... both of us.... Will you—?"

And Steve turned in time to see John Ebbarton's outstretched hand clasped by Matthew Haley. And then, in a moment Ebbarton was gone, striding swiftly toward a waiting taxi.

Steve and Gloria watched it pull away with him, and Steve noted the steamer trunk lashed on the rear, and the heavy suitcases piled beside the driver.

"Strange!" he muttered. And at Gloria's question, he told her of what he had overheard in the back study the day before.

She shuddered. "It—it's so horrible, Steve! We used to know John Ebbarton so very well. Until—father always thought he was abusing Julia. That he—was tired of her. Julia has always been so swell, but so damned unlucky. Even to the—last. I was always awfully fond of both of them, but I liked Julia better...."

She shuddered, clung closer to Steve, as they waited for Matthew Haley. "It's too bad, I think, that John Ebbarton couldn't have gone away—before Julia died. I can't help but think he tried to hound her—make her return to him. She wasn't looking well before—before it happened."

Steve grinned. "Silly! You're just nervous—over-tired. Forget the whole thing, if you can, Gloria. I'll fix you a hot drink when we get home...."

But Steve Wayne, as he tried to comfort the girl, hoped that his voice carried more confidence than he felt.

THE clock in the Haley library ticked on relentlessly, just as the clock in Morgan Bezak's apartment had ticked while measuring the moments of Belzak's life. The hour was nine-thirty. Steve Wayne paced slowly down the corridor, stepped over the library threshold, and stood staring.

The room contained only one occupant. Matthew Haley sat there in a straight-backed chair before the huge brick fireplace—sat with his head bowed in his hands, his eyes closed, his graying hair gleaming dully in the light of the bridge-lamp behind him. His lips were mumbling words, and the words, in this house of death, seemed strangely out of place, strangely macabre.

"Our Father who art in Heaven... hallowed be Thy name...."

Steve stood motionless, listening, scowling. Mechanically he pulled the glowing cigarette from his lips and held it in a dangling hand. The smoke from the white cylinder curled upward slowly, flattening out as it reached the ceiling; and Matthew Haley's droning voice continued to send up its prayer.

"...and forgive us our trespasses, as we forgive those who...."

The voice died to a whisper and became silent. Haley lifted his head, made a soft sighing sound. Then he saw Steve and stiffened guiltily, as if ashamed of himself. Steve paced forward, pulled up a chair, and sat down.

"You've thought over what I told you, Mr. Haley?"

Haley stared, moved his head up and down slowly. "I've thought about it, but—but I can't think of a single person."

"Think again. Someone, somewhere, has a grudge against you. That's the only lead we can work on."

"But I tell you, I don't know any such man."

Steve thought of John Ebbarton, and scowled. He wet the end of his cigarette and sucked on it with tight lips. Everything depended on Haley; yet the man had spent the whole day pacing helplessly about the house, refusing to speak unless spoken to. He was afraid; that was obvious. His face had grown pale; his eyes were red and watery; even now he was trembling and gripping the chair-arms with gaunt, bloodless hands.

"What did Moody say? Anything?"

"No, nothing," Haley mumbled. "He—he said he didn't know what to think. He and his men took Mrs. Ebbarton away, and he promised to come back tomorrow."

"And you can't think of a single person who might want to do you harm?"

"No—I can't."

Steve scowled again and studied the man intently. Maybe Haley was lying, but the possibility seemed remote. The fear in those eyes was too genuine; the haggard, strained expression of that tired face was no mere mask.

"You'd better go to bed," Steve said quietly.

Haley stood up as if welcoming the suggestion.

"Is—is my daughter in bed?"

"Half an hour ago."

"Very well then," Haley mumbled. "I—I can do nothing by staying up. I—good-night, Wayne."

STEVE sat alone, listening to the monotonous tick of the clock. He heard Haley walk slowly down the corridor and climb the stairs to the floor above. The silence of the house magnified every footstep, every creak of the floor. A door opened, closed dully. Then the silence was complete.

Steve stood up, turned out the light, and sat down again. He had no intention of going to bed; not yet anyway. Whoever had murdered Belzak and Mrs. Ebbarton would undoubtedly aim the next blow at someone else closely associated with Haley. Perhaps it would not happen tonight or even tomorrow night, but it would certainly happen eventually. There was nothing to be gained by going to bed, going to sleep, and waking in the morning to find a third horrible victim with its throat ripped open and the blood drained from its veins.

The clock ticked on endlessly, counting seconds into minutes, minutes into eternities. Steve took a cigarette and box of matches from his pocket, then scowled, thrust the matches back, and chewed on the cigarette without lighting it. No sound at all invaded Haley's big house. The place was a monstrous tomb, still and dark. The servants, four of them in all, had retired long ago to their quarters in the left wing. Upstairs, Gloria Haley and her father were asleep in their rooms—or at least trying to sleep. More than an hour had passed since Haley had gone upstairs.

Steve stood up, frowning. The business of waiting was enough to tighten any man's nerves, especially the nerves of a man who preferred action to aimless suspense. He put a hand in his pocket, brought out a small circular flashlight. Holding the light down and cupping it with his palm, so that its glow played over the carpet in front of him, he paced silently into the corridor. It would do no harm, and might do some good, to have a look at Haley's house while its occupants were asleep. Houses sometimes possessed souls of their own.

He moved noiselessly down the corridor, past the wide staircase. Glancing up at the well of gloom above, he thought of Gloria Haley lying asleep in her bed, and felt suddenly grateful that he had obeyed the impulse to remain in Boston. The girl needed protection. She could not get it from her father; that was sure. Matthew Haley preferred to put his trust in the Lord. That was all right, too—but Steve Wayne believed a loaded revolver, a pair of tough fists, and a fast-working brain were necessary in this case.

He prowled past the staircase, and his flashlight shone dully on a closed door at the end of the passage. The door led to the kitchen. He moved toward it. Then he stood stock still, his feet glued to the carpet and his lips clamped shut on the unlighted cigarette which protruded between them.

At the top of the staircase a floor-board had creaked ominously. Slow footsteps were audible in the upstairs corridor!

For ten seconds Steve stood rigid, listening. Then his eyes narrowed triumphantly, his lips curled. The suspense was done with now; it was a time for action, swift and decisive. The fiend responsible for Belzak's death, and the death of Matthew Haley's intended wife, had blundered, had been fool enough to return before the hue and cry had subsided!

Noiselessly Steve gained the foot of the staircase and began to ascend. His groping hand slid upward along the smooth bannister; his other hand slipped into his pocket, released the flashlight, and closed over a small automatic. If it came to a showdown, Steve Wayne knew how to use that automatic—had used it before, with deadly results, in emergencies such as this!

Halfway up the stairs he stopped, stood listening again. No sound was audible above, but after a ten-second interval of ugly silence, a significant noise came from the far end of the upstairs hall. It was hard to tabulate, that noise. It sounded like the muffled thud of bare feet parading over a wooden floor.

Steve climbed warily, revolver ready in case he needed it. He thought grimly of the horrible deaths which had overtaken the killer's two victims, and the thought caused his fingers to tighten viciously around the gun-butt. Then he reached the head of the staircase and stood motionless, trying vainly to see through the pall of darkness which enshrouded the upper corridor.

THE sound of naked feet had ceased.

The corridor was still as a vault. Slowly, deliberately Steve moved down it, staring straight ahead of him and hugging the wall.

He traversed half the length of the black passage before he

stopped again; then he stiffened, jerked his revolver up, and stood trembling. Something, some unseen, unnamable shape, had moved in the darkness ahead of him, creating a soft whisper which was almost no sound at all. That whisper was the almost inaudible sigh of breath emanating from human lips.

Steve's eyes narrowed, grew hard. Slowly he snaked a hand into his pocket and brought out the tiny flashlight. He set himself. The light snapped on, stabbing a pale ocher shaft through the dark.

Steve stood stiff, then, and sucked air through his curled lips. The flashlight's eye revealed a crouching, bare-footed figure not more than ten paces distant. Even as the light struck it, the figure straightened and whirled, glaring savagely into Steve's face. Steve saw the man's contorted features, recognized them. The man's hand was still half extended toward the door of Matthew Haley's room.

There was no hesitation. A growl of triumph welled from Steve's throat as he hurtled forward. He made no attempt to use the revolver in his hand; he wanted the killer alive. The man made a desperate effort to escape. Violently he leaped backward, pawing the wall to steady himself. Then he was down, locked in the crushing embrace of Steve's arms—down and writhing, fighting furiously to free himself.

He was no weakling. He knew tricks, used them. Sharp teeth sank into Steve's shoulder, imbedding themselves in agonized flesh. A stiff forefinger jabbed up with lightning speed and would have found a mark in Steve's throat if Steve had not lunged sideways the moment before contact. Sullenly, silently the killer strove to free himself and escape, while his hot breath assailed Steve's nostrils and his wiry body turned and twisted with snake-like rapidity.

Then he made a mistake. In the midst of his efforts he lay suddenly still, feigning defeat only to bring his knee up with crushing force and bury it in Steve's groin. Steve grunted, bent double with pain. The killer leaped erect, hesitated, swung his naked foot back to kick viciously at Steve's face.

Steve's hands shot out and clamped around the bare ankle. A

single upward thrust threw the man off balance. He stumbled, went down in a grotesque heap. Steve's clenched fist ground into that snarling mouth even before the twisted head slapped the floor. A long sigh welled from the killer's lips, and he lay still, moaning.

Steve struggled erect, then, and stood swaying, breathing in gasps. A full minute passed before he stooped and groped for the fallen flashlight; then he clicked the light on and looked both ways along the corridor. The door of Matthew Haley's room was still closed; so was the door of the adjoining room, in which Gloria lay asleep. Steve scowled, walked to the first door and stood listening. No sound came from within. Evidently the noise of conflict had not penetrated that heavy barrier, or else Haley's weariness and run-down condition had caused the man to sleep abnormally well.

But not so with Haley's daughter. The adjoining door opened while Steve was pacing back to the slumped shape on the floor. He turned abruptly, flashlight held rigid. In the doorway the girl stood facing him, staring at him fearfully.

She came forward slowly, indecision and fright stamped on her face. No doubt she had heard every separate sound of the disturbance, and had waited helplessly for the sounds to identify themselves. She was trembling now, as Steve's hand found her arm to steady her. Her white silk pajamas made her look like something unreal, fantastic. She turned a pale, strained face toward the thing on the floor and said almost inaudibly:

"What—what is it, Steve?"

Steve hesitated, then said deliberately: "Nothing. Nothing for you to worry about."

"But—"

"I'll take care of it, downstairs. Go back to bed."

Gloria took a step forward and looked down into the upturned face of the man who had attempted to invade her father's room. Steve pulled his flashlight away too slowly. She saw the face, recognized it, stiffened fearfully. It was a bloody face now, its mouth crushed and swollen, its eyes dilated. Not pretty to look at.

Devils in the Dark 19

"Mannix—" she said slowly. "Steve, it's Mannix—"

STEVE nodded grimly. The man on the floor was Mannix, the butler, the man who had served Matthew Haley for years. He had been the last man open to suspicion, had seemed utterly harmless. It was unbelievable, but—

"Go back to bed," Steve ordered again, more firmly. "You can't do anything. None of us can, until Moody gets here in the morning. I'll take care of this."

He pushed past her and bent down, lifting the butler's limp body in his arms. Deliberately he walked down the corridor, leaving the girl to stand and stare at him. At the head of the stairs he turned, looked back, then scowled and descended to the lower floor. Mannix was a dead weight, unconscious.

Steve carried him into the library, dumped him into a chair, and turned on a light. There was nothing particularly vicious about the man's appearance. His plump body was soft and limp, his face battered and bruised. But it was better to take precautions and make the man secure. Only a short while ago he had been fighting like a madman; he might do so again at the first opportunity.

Steve strode into the hall then, and turned on more lights. Still scowling, he paced into the kitchen and look around him, seeking something with which to bind the butler's arms and legs. There was no proof, yet, that Mannix had murdered Morgan Belzak and Mrs. Ebbarton; but circumstantial evidence was sufficient to turn the man over to the police.

A thick coil of rope, evidently a clothesline, hung from a nail in the corner. Steve took it, carried it back to the library. With no attempt to be gentle, he jerked the butler's legs together and bound them, passing the rope several times around the chair-legs. Then he secured the man's arms, stood back, and stared grimly into the still unconscious face.

And then he forgot Mannix, forgot the affair of the upstairs corridor, and stood utterly rigid. In his ears jangled a sound which struck fear to his heart and caused his eyes to widen with abnormal quickness.

The sound came from the rear of the house, from the direction of the servants' quarters. Like a living entity it shrilled through the corridor, eating its way into the room where Steve stood.

It was a lurid scream of absolute terror, and it came from a woman's lips.

CHAPTER FOUR

DEVIL IN THE DARK

*F*OR *TEN* seconds that scream of terror left Steve helpless. He stared mutely at Mannix, stared at the door leading to the corridor. Dully he realized that he had guessed wrong, made a terrible mistake. Next moment he was in the hall, running recklessly toward the kitchen.

The scream was not repeated, and the grim silence of the house drove caution into Steve's tormented mind before he had traversed the corridor's length. Reaching the kitchen, where he had left a light burning less than five minutes ago, he advanced warily, tensely. His hand was no longer trembling when it reached out to open the door leading to the servants' quarters. His eyes were narrowed, unblinking, his lips drawn tight in a downward scowl.

The narrow passage extending before him was lightless and he paced down it without touching the light-switch in the wall. Then he stopped, aware that the silence was no longer complete. A vague, unnamable sound emanated from the darkness ahead of him. He moved forward slowly, noiselessly; and the sound increased in volume as he neared its source.

No faintest ray of light relieved the blackness of the passage. The place was dead, lifeless, except for that significant sound. And the sound itself was hideous, ugly, suggestive of things better left alone. Somewhere ahead, in the dark, an animal was feeding hungrily—or was it an animal? Steve did not know. Grimly he advanced, striving to see what lay before him.

He came upon the thing before he expected to. Came upon it abruptly, and would have stumbled headlong into the room where the horror was being enacted, had he not caught himself in time. Prowling along the passage, feeling his way with an outstretched hand, he encountered an open doorway. His groping hand, deprived of the support of the wall, lunged into empty space and threw him off balance. He steadied himself by gripping the sides of the door-frame. Then his gaze focused on the room's contents, and he dragged a quick, rasping breath through his teeth.

The room was a small one, dimly lighted by pale moon-glow emanating from a narrow window. An iron bed angled out from the corner, its white-enameled posts and white sheets gleaming dully in the pale illumination. Beside the bed and half crouched, a black-robed shape loomed out in strange contrast. And the black-robed thing was feeding.

The thing did not turn. Evidently it had not heard the muffled sounds accompanying Steve's impromptu entrance. It was concerned only with the limp lifeless shape beneath it. That shape was a woman's body.

Steve stared, horrified. Dully he realized that he was too late; the horror had already been enacted; the woman on the bed, half naked, her nightgown ripped half off and her body exposed to the fiend's attack, was dead—mercifully so. And the black-robed monster who bent above her, his vile lips sucking the hot blood from her mangled throat, was the monster who had murdered Morgan Belzak and Mrs. Ebbarton. No other answer was possible.

Steve's hand plunged jerkily into his pocket, seeking the revolver which lay there. He had witnessed horrible things before, but this was unbelievable, fantastic. He took a step forward, dragged the gun out. His whole body was shaking; his hand, holding the weapon, refused to be still. Savagely, gutturally he rasped out the first words that came to his lips.

"Damn you, stop it! *Stop it!*"

The words had the effect of a whiplash. Like a monstrous bat the black-robed shape lunged clear of the bed, whirling on bent legs. For a split second the thing stood rigid. Its face was masked in shadow; its eyes smouldered like twin flames. Then a vicious hissing sound burst from its curled lips. With uncanny quickness the killer hurled himself forward.

Steve's gun belched once, then was rammed sideways. The bullet hit its mark, yet the murderer did not falter. White hands clawed at Steve's throat, hurling him backward. Gasping with amazement, he reeled into the wall, both fists beating a wild tattoo on the fiend's face. An odor of fresh blood assailed his nostrils, eating its way into his throat, choking him. He was fighting for his life and knew it—fighting with a monster who was human in form only. Any ordinary killer would have respected the deadly menace of a loaded revolver, would have cringed from it in fear. This black-robed being had not even hesitated, had flung himself forward so quickly, so furiously, that Steve had been caught off guard, stunned with amazement.

Now those gaunt hands were clawing Steve's face, drawing blood from torn flesh. That vile throat uttered deep, guttural growls like the rumblings of an enraged animal. Steve's clenched fists drove savagely, desperately into the fiend's chest and stomach, without effect.

Even as he fought, Steve realized that death was but a matter of moments. The room magnified every sound, hurling a torrent of noise into the corridor, just as it had hurled that first scream of terror from the lips of the woman who now lay dead on the bed. Locked in the monster's embrace, Steve stumbled backward, crashing violently against the bed-end, upsetting a small table which stood there with an unlighted lamp on it. His flailing legs caught in the rungs of a chair, upending it with a crash. He went down in a twisted heap, still fighting desperately, hopelessly, as the black-robed one fell upon him.

Then another sound filled the room, and over the monster's shoulder Steve saw a rigid shape standing in the doorway. The shape was a woman's—one of Matthew Haley's servant-girls. Her eyes were wide with horror, her hands uplifted as if to ward off the sight of the mangled victim on the bed and the robed horror in whose embrace Steve struggled. Wild shrieks rose from the woman's gaping mouth, drowning the guttural sounds of triumph which came from the monster's throat.

The grip on Steve's throat relaxed. Abruptly the black-robed fiend turned, stiffened. The next moment he was standing erect, snarling. Evidently the mind in that inhuman body was a cunning one, cunning enough to know that the tumult in the murder room had aroused the rest of the house. Ignoring Steve, the monster leaped toward the woman in the doorway. A vicious hand hurled the woman sideways. The doorway was suddenly full of a monstrous black shape; then it was empty again. The killer was gone.

THE woman was still screaming when Steve groped erect and stood swaying on braced legs. That hoarse screaming was music in Steve's ears. It had saved his life, saved him from the hideous death which had overtaken the pitiful thing on the bed. Sick at heart, nauseated by the stench of blood which clung to him, he stumbled into the corridor. His groping fingers found a light-switch; he walked unsteadily down the passage, realizing that his actions were merely mechanical and would avail nothing.

The monster had entered Matthew Haley's house without being intercepted.

Doubtlessly he had left the same way. Without hope of success, Steve paced to the end of the corridor. An open door lay before him. He stood on the threshold and stared out into darkness, his fists clenched, his lips tight. The darkness was empty. The black-robed fiend was gone.

Slowly Steve walked back to the murder room. A light was burning, and the servant-woman was standing near the death-bed, staring mutely. Steve moved to the bed and looked down, then looked away again. He knew that the woman expected him to say something, but there was nothing to say. The near-naked body on the bed was the body of the Hungarian girl who had said, not long ago: "Maybe you don't believe in vampires, but I do. I've lived where they are...."

Lived where they are! The words tortured Steve's memory. This pitiful thing on the bed, this girl named Olga something, had believed in a superstition. Now her own lifeless body, horribly mutilated and half drained of blood, presented grim proof that her beliefs had not been entirely wrong. The vampire-monster had struck thrice. Who would be his next victim?

Steve turned away and walked slowly to the door, motioning

the servant-woman to follow him. The woman said feebly:

"What—what was it, sir? Oh God, what was it? I was asleep and I woke up thinkin' I heard a scream. Then I lay there, listenin', and after a long time I heard noises in Olga's room, and I got up to see what was wrong, and—"

Steve stood still, confronting her. The words "Go back to bed" came to his lips, and he stifled them. It was not safe, now, to send anyone back to bed.

"How many more servants sleep in the house?" he demanded grimly.

"None, sir. Mrs. Pelky, the housekeeper, she said she wouldn't sleep here tonight under any conditions, after what happened to Mrs. Ebbarton. She's staying in John's room up over the garage. John's the chauffeur, and it's his night off, so he's gone home to his folks."

"You and Olga were the only ones in the servants' quarters?"

"Yes, sir. Me and—and Olga. Oh my God, sir—I can't stay here now! After lookin' at what happened to her—"

"You'd better come with me," Steve said firmly.

Deliberately he strode down the corridor to the kitchen, with the woman trailing close behind him. The light in the kitchen was still burning; the room was empty. Closing the connecting door, he entered the main corridor leading to the front rooms. At the foot of the central staircase he stopped, looked up, frowned.

"Wait here," he said stiffly. "I'll be down in a moment with Miss Haley and her father. There'll be no more sleeping tonight."

Quickly he ascended the stairs and turned on a light in the upper hall, noting with relief that the doors of the bedrooms at the far end were closed. Stopping before the door of Gloria Haley's room, he knocked softly and waited impatiently for a response. Probably the girl was asleep. Certainly no sounds from the servants' quarters had penerated to this portion of the house to disturb her.

He knocked again and said quietly: "It's Steve. Open the door, Gloria." There was a sound of a bed creaking, then soft footsteps. The door opened slowly and he looked into the tense, frightened face of Matthew Haley's daughter.

"What is, it Steve? What's happened?"

He hesitated, said evenly: "Nothing. That is, nothing much. But I want you and your father to come downstairs."

She stared at him, evidently aware that he was lying for her benefit. He put a firm hand on her arm, returned her gaze without flinching, then said softly: "Better put a dressing gown or something over those pajamas," and turned away.

The door of Matthew Haley's room was but a few paces distant. He strode toward it, knocked. After a moment he scowled, knocked and knocked again. No answering sound came from within.

He knocked a fourth time, then put a hand on the knob and turned it. The door opened when he pushed. He stood on the threshold, stared into the lightless interior and said curtly:

"Haley!"

Then he realized that something was wrong. Quickly he felt for the light-switch, found it, and stood blinking in the sudden glare. His gaze encountered an empty bed with sheets thrown back in disarray. The room was empty. Matthew Haley was gone!

CHAPTER FIVE

ONE MORE CORPSE

STEVE'S FACE lost color. Slowly he paced into Haley's room and stared around him, seeking some explanation of the man's disappearance. The bed had been slept in; that was certain. Yet the room contained no signs of violence. To all appearances Haley had retired for the night, then gotten up again and gone out. But where? Why?

Steve walked around the room, examined the bed, opened the closet door and peered past the lineup of suits hanging there. He strode to the single window and put a hand on the latch, satisfying himself that the window was locked—on the inside. Haley had not departed that way. Couldn't, anyway, unless he possessed uncanny athletic ability. The window overlooked a sheer drop of twenty feet to the ground!

Baffled, Steve moved out of the room. Gloria Haley was walking silently toward him, a heavy blue kimono wrapped tightly around her slim form. She saw the scowling expression of his face and spoke anxiously.

"Steve—"

He interrupted her curtly. "Your father's taken himself for a walk. Come downstairs."

Bewildered, she allowed herself to be led along the corridor and down the wide staircase to where the servant-woman was standing uneasily in the lower hall near the library door. Steve glanced at the door and remembered suddenly that he had left Mannix, the butler, bound to a chair in the room beyond. Striding to the threshold, he saw that the butler had not moved, had in fact, apparently resigned himself to his fate, and was sitting wearily with his eyes shut. He did not look up when the two women entered the room.

Steve faced the women grimly. They were a responsibility now, a handicap. He could not leave them alone in the house, after what had happened to the Hungarian girl. There was no telling when that black-robed fiend of darkness would return. No telling what abnormal powers the monster possessed.

Yet Matthew Haley had to be found. Fear had undoubtly caused Haley to abandon his room and seek the questionable safely of the outside. Safety? Even now the man might be wandering about the grounds or tramping the nearby streets, where his peril was infinitely greater!

A telephone lay on the library table. Steve strode to it, picked it up, worked the dial savagely with a rigid forefinger. He waited a long while for an answer, and glanced at Mannix while he waited. The butler was awake, staring at him sullenly, resentfully.

A voice came over the wire, and Steve said curtly: "Mollison there?"

The voice belonged to the deskman. Mollison—Captain Mollison of Headquarters, LaRonge Street—came to the phone a moment later and said quietly: "Yes?"

"Wayne speaking," Steve grunted. "Steve Wayne, at the Haley place. In need of help, Bob. There's been another murder."

Mollison made a rumbling sound in his throat, and Steve drew a mental picture of the man's face. It would be hard, inflexible under a mop of iron-gray hair, and Mollison would be scowling, pushing lean fingers through that gray mop. The newspapers had made a punching-bag of Mollison's department lately.

The words, "All right. I'll send a car over!" rasped into Steve's ear.

He lowered the phone and turned again to comfort Gloria Haley and the servant-woman. Gloria was sitting rigid, staring. She had not known about the affair in the servant's quarters. Steve's grim enunciation of the words "another murder" had caused the blood to ebb from her face.

But he had no intention of explaining, yet. Methodically he

paced to the butler's chair and reached down to test the man's bonds, satisfying himself that they had not been loosened during the past half hour. Just where Mannix fitted into the puzzle he was not sure; but it was better to take no chances.

And it was better to take no chances on the possible return of the black-robed monster. Grimly Steve strode to the nearest of the library windows, made sure it was locked, then walked to each of the others and tested them, too. Satisfied that no intruder could enter except by the door, he locked it, put the key in his pocket, and lowered himself into a chair near the fireplace.

"There'll be some men coming from Headquarters," he said quietly. "We'll wait."

Strangely enough, neither Gloria nor the servant-woman had anything to say. For a moment it seemed that Gloria would blurt out the questions which were certainly burning on her lips, but instead she sat motionless and stared straight ahead of her, as if realizing the seriousness of the occasion. The servant-woman looked from Steve to Mannix and back again, and seemed to be striving desperately to control her emotions.

Steve volunteered nothing. His thoughts were centered on Matthew Haley and the nameless fiend who had murdered the Hungarian girl. They were not comforting thoughts. Giving voice to them would not erase that pallid expression of fear from Gloria's face, nor remove the hunted glare from the other woman's wide eyes. Silence was the best cure—silence and patience.

In the end his patience was rewarded. A bell droned in the hall, announcing the arrival of Mollison's men. He stood up, unlocked the library door, and paced down the corridor. A moment later he was giving orders to the two uniformed men who confronted him. Then he returned to the library, put both hands on Gloria Haley's arms, and said evenly:

"There's nothing to be afraid of. Mollison's men will stay with you until morning. They'll take care of Mannix, and if that other damned thing comes back to do more murder, they'll take care of that, too!"

"You—you're going to leave me, Steve?"

"I'm going to find your father."

She stared at him anxiously and reached out to hold him back. Then she regained control of herself, said in a mechanical voice: "All right, Steve," and sat motionless in her chair, watching him as he walked away.

He glanced at the clock on the mantel as he went out. The hour was one-thirty.

SIX hours later he had achieved nothing. There had been no lead to follow, nothing except the bewildering knowledge that Matthew Haley had climbed out of bed in the middle of the night and vanished.

Steve Wayne had searched the house and grounds and prowled up and down the streets of the neighborhood. He had talked to the driver of an owl cab parked near an all-night drugstore three blocks from the Haley home. But there had been no clue. Matthew Haley had simply vanished.

Now it was seven-thirty and the night was over. Wearily he made an end of his futile search and cursed himself for a fool. What had he expected? To find Haley walking the streets mumbling prayers? To find the man huddled in some obscure doorway, shivering with terror? Haley might be frightened, but not to that extent! It was obvious now that the man had gone to some premeditated destination, perhaps to the home of a friend. But where?

Steve stood on the corner of Cypress and Verne Streets, half a mile from the Haley home, and looked both ways for a cab. A cafeteria was open on the other side of the square. He went into it, ordered coffee and a sandwich, and gulped the food without wanting it. Fifteen minutes later, suffering from fatigue and a vicious headache, he paced along the sidewalk of upper Verne Street, toward Matthew Haley's big house.

He stopped then, and stood staring at a stoop-shouldered figure shuffling across the street toward him. His eyes widened; he made a guttural sound in his throat and scowled blackly.

The stoop-shouldered figure was Matthew Haley!

For a moment Steve's astonishment paralyzed him. He gaped, unable to realize that his search was over, that it had ended precisely where it had begun—at Haley's own home. Then he advanced slowly, staring with wide eyes. Judging from the appearance of Haley's crumpled clothes and from the slow, leaden scuff of his feet as he walked, the man had spent the night in the open—had not gone to the home of a friend, after all. He looked tired, helpless. Looked as if he were suffering from a severe hangover after an all-night's drunk. And there was something wrong with one of his shoulders. It seemed abnormally large, swollen.

Steve hung back, suppressing a violent desire to stride forward and blurt out the man's name. Haley had not seen him, had not looked up. Without once turning around, he scuffled sluggishly up the cement walk of his own home and climbed the steps. He did not ring the bell, but produced a ring of keys from a pocket of his crumpled coat and fumbled with them awkwardly. When he got the door open at last, he paced over the threshold like a dead man, leaving the door open wide.

Steve followed cautiously, his eyes still clouded with bewilderment, his mouth twisted at the corners in a fixed frown. He did not understand, did not pretend to; but not once did he consider interrupting Haley's slow progress.

Wearily the man proceeded down the corridor toward the library door, looking neither to right nor left. He apparently had no intention of stopping. His destination was the staircase, and probably his own bedroom on the floor above. But the library door was half open when he came abreast of it, and before he could pace past, the door was jerked wide and Gloria Haley stepped out.

The girl stopped, rigid, gazing first at her father, then at Steve, who was pacing down the corridor not ten strides behind him. She spoke just one word—"Father!"—and spoke it in a whisper. There was no relief in her voice. Nothing but awe and amazement. She, too, did not understand.

But unlike Steve, she did not wait to see what her father would do. Her outstretched hands caught his arms, holding him, pulling him toward her. Matthew Haley looked wearily into her face and said dully, without emotion:

"What—what's the matter?"

She drew him inside, and Steve followed. A police officer—one of Mollison's men—leaned against the library table, gazing with narrowed eyes. Mannix, the butler, was asleep in his chair near the fireplace. The servant-woman was gone, probably back to her own room to get some rest now that the danger of darkness was over.

The police officer looked at Steve and said: "What's happened to Mr. Wayne?" Steve said nothing, merely stared at Gloria as she forced her father into a chair and did little things to make him comfortable. Turning, she said anxiously:

"Where was he, Steve? Where did you find him?"

"I didn't."

"But—"

Steve moved forward and put both hands on Haley's shoulders, then withdrew one hand abruptly as Haley winced with pain.

"Where've you been, Mr. Haley?"

Haley looked up, mumbled thickly: "I—I don't know."

"No idea, hey?"

"I—don't remember. This house was driving me mad; I just had to get away from it. Where I went I don't know."

"You're pretty badly banged up," Steve observed. "How'd that happen?"

"I must have—fallen."

STEVE scowled suspiciously. His hand came to rest on the swollen shoulder and would have drawn aside the coat which covered it. But Haley stiffened with unexpected abruptness and dragged the probing hand away.

"It's nothing—only a bruise. Leave me alone. I'm tired. I want to go to bed and—"

Haley's head slumped down on his chest. Gloria moved toward him, stopped, and looked at Steve with a worried expression on her face.

"Do you think he's all right?" she said quickly. "Shall I call a doctor?"

"He needs sleep," Steve shrugged. "Takes a lot out of a man his age staying up all night."

Then he turned away, fearful that she might read his thoughts. They were unpleasant thoughts, caused by several significant things that refused to pass unnoticed. In the first place, that injured shoulder of Haley's needed explaining, and could not be explained away by a mere, "I must have fallen." Beneath Haley's coat that shoulder was bandaged heavily; and no man would have taken the trouble to wrap heavy bandages around a bruise.

Another thing: Haley was wearing shoes that did not fit him. They were not his own shoes; they were a couple of sizes too large. That, too, needed some explanation.

Steve leaned against the fireplace and stared at the man in the chair, attempting to unravel the questions and put plausible answers to them. The answers would not come from Haley himself; that was certain. Already the man was asleep, or feigning sleep. The answers would have to come from some other source. But where?

He found out a moment later. A door opened and closed in the hall, and heavy boots beat a rapid tattoo along the floor, toward the library. Turning abruptly, Steve stared into the tense face of the second of Mollison's men. The detective stood straight and stiff on the threshold, gripping the sides of the door-frame with both hands. His face was paler than it should have been. From the glare of his unblinking eyes it was evident that he had seen something not pretty to look at.

He came forward quickly and began to talk before he reached Steve's side. The words were harsh, strained, indicative of over-worked emotions.

"You'd better come with me, Mr. Wayne. Somethin'—well, somethin's happened. I been prowlin' around, and I took a look in the garage, and found—"

The word "garage" caused Steve to peer sharply at Matthew Haley. Especially at Haley's ill-fitting shoes. He had been trying to place those shoes, trying to decide what type of man would be apt to own them. They were fashioned of coarse-grained black leather, with solid heels and unusually thick soles.

Garage? That was enough! Triumphantly, Steve swung on the man from Headquarters and said: "Show me."

Then, ignoring Gloria Haley's stare, he followed the man into the corridor.

THE garage was a square cement structure about a hundred yards distance from the house proper. Striding down the gravel path, with the police officer pacing grimly at his side Steve remembered what the servant-woman had told him in the room where the girl named Olga had been murdered. Last night had been the chauffeur's night off. The housekeeper, Mrs. Pelky, had slept in the chauffeur's room, preferring its comparative isolation to the sinister threat of the Haley household.

The garage door was unlocked. Mollison's man entered, leading the way across a smooth floor, down a narrow aisle between the running-boards of two large cars which gave silent indication of Haley's financial security. A wooden stairway extended upward at the rear. The detective stood aside, allowing Steve to ascend first.

The door at the top was closed. Steve opened it, stepped quietly into the room beyond. Then he stopped abruptly and said in a low voice: "Good Lord!" And Mollison's man, entering behind him, closed the door and leaned against it, methodically lighting a cigarette.

The room was a small one, decently furnished with furniture evidently carried over from the main house. A three-quarter bed stood against one wall, a small oil-stove against another. A heavy oak table, with chairs grouped around it, loomed up in the center. In one of the chairs, stiffly upright, sat a thick-shouldered, dark-complexioned man who was evidently the chauffeur, John. And the man was a prisoner.

Ropes encircled his ankles, binding them securely to the chair-legs. Other ropes bound his arms behind him, where there was less possibility of his working them loose. Steel handcuffs held his wrists. Grimly silent, he returned Steve's bewildered gaze; and there was a challenging glint in the man's dark eyes which advertised a fiery temper behind that foreign-looking face.

But that was not all—not nearly all. Steve's gaze traveled to the bed and clung there, refusing to shift away. The bed was occupied. A woman lay there, hunched in a position of silent agony,

Devils in the Dark 35

her wide eyes gaping up at the low ceiling, her hands clenched fiercely on the crumpled bed-clothes.

She did not move when Steve paced toward her and bent over her. She could not. Her half-stripped body was stiff with rigor-mortis. Her ghastly white throat was torn horribly, just as the throats of Morgan Belzak, Mrs. Julia Ebbarton, and Olga had been torn.

The black-robed killer had claimed another victim. The woman on the bed was Mrs. Pelky, the housekeeper, and she was dead.

Steve stared down at her, unable to speak. There was no need to ask questions—not even mental ones. The monster's trademark was all too evident, and this time nothing had interrupted the fiend in his blood feast. Judging from the whiteness of the woman's body, nearly every drop of blood had been drained from it, through that hideous gash in the throat. The killer had come here after escaping from the death-room of the Hungarian girl—had come here, found Mrs. Pelky alone, and fallen upon her with the same obscene hunger which had marked his other attacks.

Who would be next?

Shuddering despite every effort to control his emotions, Steve turned to face Mollison's man and the prisoner in the chair. He understood the method of Mrs. Pelky's death, yes, but the presence of the chauffeur was still a mystery. Obviously Mollison's man was responsible for the ropes and handcuffs—but why?

The Headquarters man answered for himself. Advancing slowly, he pulled the sodden cigarette from his lips and glared at the prisoner, then said grimly:

"That's what I found when I came in here—that woman lyin' there on the bed. It gave me the horrors I'm tellin' you, but I took a good look at her and then gave the place the once-over. Then this guy came in, kind of slow and careful like, and I figured the best thing to do was hold onto him until I could bring you over here."

The prisoner said nothing. Steve glanced at him, scowled, and said slowly:

"Why didn't you bring him to the house?"

"Well, I was goin' to. But he acted kind of hard-boiled, and I didn't want to take no chances. He's a wise guy, and the best thing to do with wise guys is put 'em in irons."

Steve stood over the prisoner's chair, stared down.

"You heard what he said. Anything to say?"

"What am I supposed to say?" the chauffeur snarled.

"Plenty, if you're wise."

"Well, I don't know what you're talkin' about, see? I wasn't home all night and when I got back here a little while ago, this guy jumped on me. I don't know nothin' about what happened."

Steve studied the man critically, taking in every detail of his appearance from the twisted face and massive shoulders to the long, powerful legs and large feet. Perhaps the man was lying, perhaps not. There was no way of knowing yet. But the answer lay in Steve's mind, and he was becoming increasingly sure that the answer was a correct one.

"Better take him to the house," he ordered quietly. "I'll be over later."

Mollison's man nodded and set about the business of releasing the prisoner's huge body. Gun in hand, he ordered the chauffeur to stand up, then marched him to the door. Steve waited impatiently for the door to close.

Then Steve turned and made a slow, careful examination of the room, seeking something, anything, which might add to the half-formed belief in his mind. Deliberately he inspected the table, the bed, the small bureau which stood in one corner. With almost fanatical attention to detail, he picked up two pairs of shoes from beneath the bed and studied them.

Ten minutes had passed before he opened the door and descended the stairs. Even then he did not proceed at once to the house, but walked slowly around the garage, staring intently at the ground.

Then he stopped and stood motionless. At his feet, in the soft earth beneath the single window of the upstairs room, lay the deep imprint of thick-soled shoes, toes pointing inward toward the wall. The window was half open.

Someone, within the past few hours, had climbed through that window, hung at arm's length, and dropped. Unless for some unknown reason those footprints had been planted there, they had belonged certainly to the black-robed fiend who had murdered Mrs. Pelky—yet the monster had worn no shoes at all when confronted in the room of the Hungarian girl, Olga.

Steve did not know the answer. He knew only that the footprints in the ground before him were large ones, and corresponded in size to the heavy-soled shoes which lay beneath the murder-bed upstairs in the chauffeur's room.

TWO prisoners were waiting in the library when Steve returned. One of them, the chauffeur, was standing erect beside the table, staring straight ahead of him and scowling defiantly. The other, Mannix the butler, still sat near the fireplace, eyes half shut and head sunk on his chest. Matthew Haley was asleep in his chair. Gloria and the two Headquarters men looked at Steve expectantly as he entered.

There was no indecision in Steve's mind then. His plan had taken form and seemed plausible. He strode forward, glared at the chauffeur, and said grimly to Mollison's men:

"Take him to Headquarters. The charge is murder."

If the two officers were surprised, they concealed their emotions expertly. One of them tightened his grip on the chauffeur's arm and looked casually at Mannix.

"What about him?"

"I'll be responsible for him. He's just a poor fool who got himself into trouble. The chauffeur is your man."

"You'll come down to Headquarters, Mr. Wayne?"

"Later."

Mollison's men walked quietly to the door, taking their sullen prisoner with them. Mannix, leaning forward in his chair, was smiling triumphantly. Gloria Haley was staring with large eyes, as if unable to believe.

Steve laid a hand on Matthew Haley's shoulder and said evenly: "You hear, Haley? There's nothing more to fear."

Haley moved his head up and down wearily, too tired to be relieved.

Steve released him, said casually to Gloria: "You'd better take him upstairs," then turned to confront the butler.

Mannix peered at him intently, but said nothing.

Steve leaned against the table, waiting for Gloria and her father to leave the room. While he waited, he beat a soft tattoo on the table-top with the lean fingers of one hand. Was he being a fool?

Was he making mountains out of insignificant nothings, and charging recklessly along a road which might lead to more horror? He did not know.

He walked to the door and closed it, then returned and drew a chair close to the butler's face. Then he said grimly:

"Now you're going to talk."

The butler squirmed, his lips compressed, his face red. At last he said: "You—you've no right—"

Steve leaned forward. His left hand shot out and his fingers locked on the man's shirt-front. "All the right in the world, Mannix. And enough experience in this business to make tougher birds than you warble."

The butler's Adam's apple moved up and down. His cheeks drained of color. "All—anything I may know is just—just gossip, sir. Servant's talk, as you might say. Hardly worth—"

"Out with it!"

The butler wet his lips. "It—it hurts to talk about Mr. Haley, sir. I've been with him—with his family ever since I was a shaver, and my mother before me. But they do say that back, generations ago, there was some—some *vampire* blood in his family. There!"

Steve snorted audibly, disdainfully. "Good God! Evidence, man—real evidence—is what I want." He shrugged resignedly. "All right—go ahead, then. Speak your piece!"

But though Mannix with fear in his eyes and in a hushed voice, was perfectly willing to repeat a fantastic tale of Matthew Haley's great-grandmother having been under suspicion of vampirism— "and I'd like to find any authority claiming *that's* an inherited trait," gritted Steve to himself—of any substantial light on the gruesome murders, Mannix had none.

At length, after enough cross-questioning to convince himself that the butler was either a superb liar or—and this was more likely—a badly frightened and not-too-bright servant, Steve was inclined to dismiss the man.

CHAPTER SIX

In Gloria's Room

THE CLOCK on the library mantel was striking ten that night when Steve entered the room and strolled over to turn on the radio. The day had been uneventful; he had expected it to be so. Inspector Moody had come at noon, remained to talk a while, then gone away again, sending a department car later to remove the bodies of the Hungarian girl and Mrs. Pelky. Later in the afternoon Matthew Haley had come downstairs to apologize for his actions of the preceding night.

Haley was in his study now, messing about among books and papers in an apparent effort to get his mind off the events of the past hours of horror. He little knew how close he had come to being arrested as a matter of routine—how savagely Steve had argued with Inspector Moody in a successful effort to change Moody's mind. But Moody was gone now, and the house harbored only five persons: Haley, Haley's daughter, the servant-woman, Mannix, and Steve Wayne.

Steve glanced at the clock, lowered himself into a comfortable chair, and relaxed. Relaxed physically, at least. Mentally he was living in the future. In another three or four hours, perhaps less, he would know whether or not Steve Wayne was a fool. Meanwhile, the Boston Symphony Orchestra, under the capable direction of Serge Koussevitsky, was offering Erik Satie's mournful masterpiece, *Gymnopédies*. The deep, low tones were comforting, nerve-soothing.

Steve thought of Gloria Haley, and for the first time in many hours thought of her as something more than Matthew Haley's daughter. The girl was upstairs now in her own room, sleeping, with the servant-woman attending her. She had promised to come downstairs soon. He wondered if she would.

She did, even before *Gymnopédies* had reached its droning conclusion. Entering the library quietly, she came and sat close to him. She had done things to her face and hair to erase the haggard look caused by fear and lack of sleep. She wore a dark, clinging gown which made him all the more conscious of the fact that she was a woman, and not an ordinary woman. Leaning toward him, she said quietly:

"Steve—are you really sure of yourself? Do you really believe father's chauffeur did those awful things?"

Steve scowled and stopped staring at her. Turning his head to hide the expression on his face, he answered mechanically:

"Let's forget about it."

"But—"

"It's over and done with, Gloria. I'm not over-anxious to rehash it."

He stood up and leaned over the back of her chair letting his fingers move idly through her hair. It was soft hair, unbelievably soft; and the radio in the corner was whispering one of Tchaikovski's gentler themes in a mood not at all conducive to thoughts of murder. Steve leaned closer and turned the girl's head toward him.

"You're lovely," he said simply, and meant it.

Then he stiffened. Slow footsteps were audible in the corridor, and the doorway was suddenly full of Matthew Haley's stoop-shouldered form. Haley stared blinkingly, but did not advance across the threshold. In a thin voice he announced:

"I'm going to bed, you two. If you want to stay up, that's your own business—but you need sleep, Gloria. Do you hear?"

Gloria sighed patiently. "Yes, father."

"Good-night, then."

"Good-night."

The footsteps receded to the stairs, ascended slowly, and died out along the upper hall. Gloria sighed again and said softly: "I suppose I ought to humor him, Steve. He's been through so much."

She stood up, obviously waiting to be kissed. Steve drew her close to him and kissed her mechanically, casually. Already he was thinking of other things and wondering again if he had not made a bad mistake. When the girl left him he stood motionless beside the library table, staring straight ahead of him and scowling. Then he strode to the radio, turned it off, and lit a cigarette.

HALF an hour later, when he paced out of the library and ascended the stairs to his own room on the upper floor the big house was sinister with silence A light burned in the upstairs corridor—a light which he, being the last one to retire, was supposed to turn off. He left it burning.

In his own room he turned on the lamp beside the bed, closed the door quietly then sat on the side of the bed and drew a revolver from his pocket. Cigarette still dangling from his lips, he removed the clip from the gun, examined it, and replaced it. Then he put the weapon back in his pocket, stretched himself out at full length, and gazed moodily up at the ceiling.

Before the night was over he would know the answers to the many questions which confronted him. Of that he was certain. There was nothing to do now but wait.

Lying there he drew a mental plan of the house and its occupants. Mannix, the butler, would be asleep in his room in the servants' quarters, unless the man were a better actor than he had seemed to be while talking in the library a long while ago. The servant-woman had undoubtedly returned to the servants' quarters, too, and would be locked in her room, either sleeping or trying to. That left Matthew Haley and Gloria, both of whom occupied rooms here on the second floor of the main house. There was no one else—except the black-robed monster who came and went during the silent hours of darkness, committing horrible murder wherever his vile hands found a victim. Perhaps the man was even now a prisoner at headquarters, as Gloria and the others believed.

Perhaps not!

Steve blocked his cigarette in the bottom of an ash tray, lit another one, and looked at his watch. The hour was eleven-twenty, and the hands of the watch, as he gazed at them, moved with maddening sluggishness. Yet those hands would eventually lead to a brief interlude of hell—he was sure of it. The trap was laid. Everything now depended on patience, and on his ability to act quickly, decisively, when the moment of horror arrived.

No sound disturbed the utter stillness of the house. No sound at all. The lamp beside the bed threw a pale halo of light over the carpet, and the soft circle of illumination reached out dully to embrace the door which led to the corridor. Steve lay motionless, staring at the door, dragging deep lungfuls of cigarette smoke to keep himself alert.

Already he had blocked three butts and tossed them aside. Mechanically he shook a fourth cigarette out of its package.

Then it happened.

THE sound was almost no sound at all, merely the soft, distant creaking of a door. So vague was it, and so indefinite, that it seemed to have no source, seemed to be a disembodied, ghostly whisper alive in itself, as if the silence of the big house had suddenly become possessed of a soul.

But Steve had heard it—was sure he had heard it. Cautiously he lowered both feet to the floor and stood erect, gripping the end of the bed with a rigid hand. The door seemed miles away as he stared at it; yet he knew that he must reach it and reach it without making the slightest noise. Slowly, deliberately, he tiptoed toward it until his outstretched fingers curled around the knob.

He stood motionless then, every nerve alert for a repetition of the sound which had galvanized him to action. But it was not the creaking of a door that he heard; it was another sound, more significant and more sinister. Someone was moving warily, furtively along the corridor outside!

Steve's hand slid into his pocket and closed over the revolver that lay there. It was comforting, that revolver—far more comforting than the thoughts festering in his mind. He had anticipated this very thing that was happening; but reality was infinitely more vicious than anticipation. He wished suddenly that he had confided in Inspector Moody and prevailed upon Moody to remain in the house. The lone-wolf game was sometimes safer, yes—specially where silence and subtlety were needed—but if the lone wolf failed now, tonight, a woman might pay the horrible penalty for his failure!

Grimly Steve waited, listening to the rapid thumping of his own heart and the soft whisper of naked feet in the corridor beyond the door. It was a gamble. If he flung open the door and challenged the creator of those whispering foot-steps, confronting the man before he could reach Gloria Haley's room, the ordeal would be over—but nothing would be proved, no questions answered. If he waited, allowing the man to reach his objective, then a single blunder on the part of Steve Wayne would be the forerunner of a tragedy unspeakable.

He waited. One hand nursed the revolver in his pocket; the other came up jerkily to wipe the cold perspiration from his forehead.

Slowly, with hellish deliberation, the footsteps whispered past his door and continued down the hall. They would never end, it seemed; but they did end. Then for a maddening interlude of uncertainty no sound at all invaded the stillness of the house. The place stopped breathing, stopped living. An eternity passed. At the very moment when Steve's nerves threatened to crack under the strain, a key grated softly in a lock, and a door opened with a single protesting groan.

Then Steve moved. Quickly, noiselessly, he drew open the door in front of him and stepped into the corridor. At the far end of the passage, near the head of the wide staircase, the overhead light was still burning, casting gaunt shadows along the carpeted floor. The passage was empty. The door of Gloria Haley's room, ten yards distant, hung ajar. An hour ago—or was it longer?—that door had been closed!

Steve tiptoed toward it, every muscle tense, every nerve on edge. He had no time to think now, at least no time to think of anything but his own grim responsibility. Intuitively he knew what he would find when he invaded the girl's room, and he shuddered to think of what he might find if he were too late.

Revolver in hand, he advanced. Then he stopped. From the doorway ahead of his came a sound which stabbed into him with shocking abruptness, stifling the breath in his throat. It was a vibrant, high-pitched scream flung out of a woman's lips, and it was alive with terror.

Like the screech of a siren that scream shrilled through the corridor, smothering every other thing with its awful intensity. It ate into Steve's brain, numbing him, causing him to stand stiff and helpless for an eternity composed of endless seconds. Then the sinister sound died with uncanny quickness, as if a hand had closed over the lips that uttered it.

Steve leaped forward violently, sucking a great breath between clenched teeth. The doorway hung before him. He reached it, flung himself across the threshold, his free hand clawing at the doorframe to steady himself. His eyes were already wide open, staring. In the split-second interval that he stood swaying, his gaze swept every portion of the shadowy room, drinking in its contents.

The room was dark. But the light from the corridor, slanting through the open doorway, revealed enough to sap every trace of color from Steve's face. There was a bed, gleaming white against the wall. There was a black-robed shape bending over it, tittering guttural sounds which were half human and half animal—vile, throaty sounds of triumph and hungry anticipation. There was a woman on the bed, writhing silently and horribly in the grip of the monster's powerful hands.

Once again, as on that other occasion when he had faced the black-robed fiend, Steve gave voice to involuntary words of terror. The words welled from his throat without his knowing it. Viciously they rasped across the room.

"Stop it! For God's sake—"

The robed figure turned—turned with inhuman quickness, releasing its victim. Like a huge bat it swung about, arms upraised, eyes glaring in a face convulsed. Steve's fist jerked up, gripping the revolver. He took aim at the very center of that menacing mass. His finger tightened on the trigger.

But the finger did not tighten all the way. Staring into that white face, Steve knew that his suspicions had been corrrect. Like a man stricken with paralysis he stood stiff as stone, gazing into that familiar, mask-like countenance, realizing its awful significance.

Then it was too late. With a single rasping snarl of triumph, the monster was upon him.

CHAPTER SEVEN

MONSTER UNMASKED

MADNESS TOOK possession of Steve at that moment. Aware of his danger, he stumbled backward, both hands extended before him to hold the monster's lunging body at bay. That hideous black-robed shape was death itself, death incarnate. If it succeeded in accomplishing its purpose, the woman lying there on the bed, limp and unconscious, would be the next victim. Perhaps she was already dead. She had not moved since the fiend had released her—had not cried out or displayed any show of life.

Into Steve's mind came visions of the monster's other victims, their throats ripped open, their mutilated bodies drained of blood, their dead faces fixed in unchangeable expressions of utter horror. The visions came to him as visions might torment a man on the verge of death by drowning. He, himself, was drowning, in a vicious sea of madness. That white gargoyle of a face hung above him, inches away from his own. The wall had ended his stumbling retreat. The monster's gaunt hands were reaching toward him out of the folds of the black robe.

A gasping cry sobbed from Steve's lips. The revolver, now that it meant the difference between life and death, no longer lay in his fist. He had dropped it. Frantically he braced himself, hammered his knuckles against the face and chest of his adversary. Desperation had given him added strength. His blows drove the creature back, gave him an opening to lunge forward and hurl himself against the fiend's legs. The monster's thick-set body snapped backward, tumbled off balance, went down with a thud which shook the floor.

Steve found new life then. On hands and knees he staggered forward, hurled himself upon the black-robed shape before it could grope erect. His clenched fist rose and fell, missing its mark and thudding against the floor with an impact that drove a cruel stab of agony through his arm and shoulder. A powerful hand clutched at him, dragging him sideways. Locked in the monster's embrace, he rolled over and over, striving wildly to gain the uppermost position.

A chair stopped him. Hard, sharp timbers burned into his back with crushing force, throwing him into the full grip of the fiend's arms. For a moment dizziness overwhelmed him, leaving him limp and stunned. Then he looked into the very center of his assailant's contorted face, saw the triumph stenciled there. The killer's lips were parted, drooling; the sunken eyes were twin wells of hunger.

Instinct alone made Steve jerk his head sideways, twisting his exposed throat away from the attack of that murderous mouth. Instinct—and perhaps the subconscious memory of what had happened to the black fiend's other victims. But the drooling lips shot toward him again, intent on reaching their goal. Gaunt fingers groped up and locked in his hair, wrenching his head backward.

Steve did the only thing possible—jerked up a hand and clamped it squarely over the killer's drooling mouth. Touching that evil countenance was like touching something from the grave; it sent a chill of horror through him, loading him with nausea. But his effort brought results. The grip on his hair loosened; he heaved himself free with a violent twist of his shoulders. Once again he crashed into the legs of the table near the bed, and this time the table splintered under the impact, toppling with a crash.

Something hard rolled under his flailing arms then, something round and solid that gleamed before his eyes as it came to rest within reach of his hand. He groped for it even as the monster fell upon him with renewed vigor, snarling furiously and giving voice to enraged growls which reverberated viciously throughout the length and breadth of the death-room. The fiend would not be denied this time. His ghastly fingers raked Steve's face. His gaping mouth descended, lips apart and teeth gleaming.

STEVE'S hand closed desperately over the metal object which had fallen from the table. It was a box of some sort, probably a trinket-box in which Gloria Haley had kept feminine odds and ends. But it was a weapon now, and a last resort. It was life to a man on the threshold of hideous death.

Steve made one last lunge to escape the fiend's attack. The lunge was half successful; it carried him to his knees and left him free for the duration of a split second, swaying wildly as he sought to balance himself. His arm swung back, forward again. The base of the metal box crashed full into the killer's distorted face, as the face came closer with snakelike quickness.

The face receded, choking and gasping. Again and again Steve swung, hammering first with his naked fist, then with the knotted hand that held the blunt-edged weapon. Enormous vitality must have inhabited that black-robed body. The killer fell backward, striving vainly to seize the box in his clawing fingers. A dozen furious blows were needed to subdue him. Even then, with his gargoyle face battered almost beyond recognition, his hands and wrists gouged and bloody from the weapon's crushing impacts, he did not lose consciousness. It took a last deliberate blow of Steve's fist, delivered at close range with sledge-hammer force, to drive him to the floor and silence him forever.

But the ordeal was over then. Trembling in every muscle. Steve put both hands on the edge of the bed and dragged himself erect, to stand swaying like a man who had imbibed great quantifies of liquor. A full moment passed before he found strength enough to stagger along the wall and reach out a hand to the light-switch. Then, exhausted and nauseated, his clothes torn in a score of places from the savage clawing of the fiend's fingers, he leaned against the wall and gulped great mouthfuls of breath, fighting to remain conscious.

Another full minute passed before he was sufficiently sure of himself to leave the support of the wall and stumble across the carpet. He did not look down at the robed thing on the floor. He did not want to. He had seen enough of that hellish shape to last him a lifetime.

Slowly he moved to the bed and stared down at the motionless body of the monster's intended victim, and a sob of relief escaped from his swollen lips as he saw that the girl's throat was unmarked. He had not been too late. In another few seconds he might have been, for the girl's pajama jacket was ripped wide, exposing the entire upper portion of her body. But the killer had been interrupted before sinking his vile teeth in that ivory-white throat. Gloria Haley was unconscious, yes—but unharmed.

The girl's eyes opened while Steve gazed down at her. They opened slowly and remained wide, her gaze focused on the bleeding wounds in his face. But she did not speak. She seemed to be straggling wearily to remember something, to gather her thoughts together and make sense of them. For a long while she lay very still, staring up at her protector; then, apparently aware of her near-nakedness for the first time, she caught the torn front of her jacket in a trembling hand and pulled it over her. And she said slowly, hesitantly:

"Steve—that horrible thing—"

Steve glanced at the thing on the floor. He could have hidden it from her, could have covered the black-robed shape with a blue blanket which lay folded at the end of the bed. But he knew better. Gloria Haley, now, was in a semi-stupor caused by the shock of her nightmare ordeal. Her mind was not fully receptive. It was better for her to look into that ghastly countenance now, to recognize it, rather than be denied the truth until some later time when the horror would strike her with full force.

And already the girl was staring, staring intently at the black-robed shape. Her groping hand caught Steve's arm and clung there. She said slowly:

"What—is it, Steve?"

He made no answer. Deliberately he put an arm around her and helped her to sit up. He walked with her toward the thing on the floor, and stood beside her as she gazed down into the monster's upturned face.

A HEAVY shudder passed through the girl's slender body as she looked down. Slowly, like an automaton, she sunk to her knees on the carpet, her gaze riveted immovably on those battered features.

Steve watched her intently. Would she recognize them, under that hellishly clever make-up of puttied features, of dyed gray hair and other items from the makeup box? Of course—she must!

The only sound that came from her lips was a low, tremulous moan. Stooping swiftly, Steve saw the bullet-shattered shoulder, flung a blanket over that gaunt, glaring face. Long afterward he remembered how it had looked at that second, and cursed himself for a fool for even allowing the girl to glance at it.

It glared up at that last instant, without emotion. There was no life left in it. Its sunken eyes were half-open, glazed. Its pale flesh was caked with blood, gleaming scarlet and white against the background of the carpet. Obscene hunger was still indelibly printed in those ghastly features; the bloody lips were still parted, as if eager, even in death, to fasten on the throat of some unwary victim....

The girl's eyes were glazing as she sank back weakly against the pillow. Steve's jaw tightened. He went to the closet, flung something over her, then went to the house phone and called Mannix.

Speaking a few words to the butler, he left—and walked slowly down the hall toward the door of Matthew Haley's room....

Outside he paused, listening, his hand raised against the panel. There was no perceptible sound from within. His knuckles rapped sharply.

For a long moment then, he waited.

A voice, muffled, came to him. "What is it?"

Steve went in. Matthew Haley lay on the bed; his eyes bleary, his face showing signs of suffering, of tearing nerve-straining worry.

As he saw Steve, he let out a sigh that might have been of relief.

Steve said softly: "It's happened again, Mr. Haley. For the last time."

Matthew Haley trembled as if in a fit of ague. Steve spoke soothingly, yet distinctly. "You're all right, Mr. Haley. Quite all right now. Don't be afraid any longer. He's dead."

Haley muttered thickly, brokenly: "Are—are you—*sure?* It—it's not—I'm not the—?"

Steve smiled reassuringly. "No. I knew—I guessed—how worried you were. I found out about—about that strain that ran through your family. It is enough to frighten anyone."

There was a knock on the door. Mannix appeared, a steaming cup of black coffee, laced with rum, on a tray. He went out immediately. Steve gave that to Haley.

"Drink it," he ordered. And then, after a moment, he spoke quietly, "Your friend—John Ebbarton—was the killer," he said.

AFTER a moment, Haley's eyes cleared. "That—hound of hell!" he gasped.

"Yes—it would be— John Ebbarton! He was a fiend—a sadist. Drove Julia from him, though God knows I was more than glad that he did—until her death. He too was suffering under a curse, though I didn't realize it at the time. Nocturnal blood-lust. He must have known it, and tried to—to kill two birds with one stone, by cleverly disguising himself as me!"

"I was sure that it was not you whom I shot in the shoulder," Steve cut in. "Though I swear I couldn't be sure at the time. His idea of killing your partner first, after you'd had that inconsequential quarrel, then—Julia. Damned clever of him to make sure that you were well hidden every time he put in an appearance."

"God man, I—I didn't know what I was doing more than half the time, except I was sure that I was living through a hell of nightmares."

Steve nodded. "When I was sure that the killer in the Hungarian girl's room wore no shoes, and then when you came home with a pair too large for you, unable to explain your absence—it sounded too good. I smelled dope on you then. I know my narcotics, and that which I smelled, I knew was not habit-forming. I suspected then that you'd been drugged without your knowledge. Had you been guilty, and smart, you'd have had an alibi.

"Ebbarton still had you in his power when he remembered that Mrs. Pelky, the housekeeper, was sleeping alone in her room over the garage. Then—after he killed her—he fed you some antidote for the drug and sent you home, dazed, after nipping you in the shoulder with a silenced gun, and putting the chauffeur's shoes on your feet."

"Yes—but the chauffeur? You were sure—?"

"He was a stall, that's all," Steve grinned. "I figured that Ebbarton might have gotten on to my true suspicions, and I accused the chauffeur of being the killer to lull any uneasiness he might have had. But I nearly let it go too far."

"How do you mean?"

"Gloria—he was in Gloria's room—"

"My God!" Haley jumped from the bed. "Is she all right?" Frantic, stark panic was in his voice as he swept blindly toward the door.

Steve nodded, took his arm. "Do you think I'd be alive if she wasn't all right," he grinned. "And now let's go to her. I think she'd like to see you—better, maybe, than she ever did before."

A smile—one of the first that Steve ever remembered seeing there—broke over Haley's thin mouth as, guided by the steadying hand of Steve Wayne, he went down the hallway.

THE END

HUGH B. CAVE

INN OF THE SHADOW-CREATURES

Cary Booth had been forewarned of the dire peril that lay in store for him in that dark musty inn—but to a man who raced in agony before the bloodhounds of the law, no unearthly fear seemed real. He had not yet seen the ghastly, spectral shape that prowled the dim-lit hallways, lusting to bathe in the gore of its midnight butchery!...

*T*HE CONTRAST between crawling night-shadows and the lovely dark-eyed face of the girl who was staring at him startled Cary Booth.

He forgot the throbbing agony in his side and the endless weary miles of trudging that had intensified that agony, until he had all but flung his weary body into the deep grass by the roadside. Forgot, too, for a moment at least, the black shadows that had writhed so long in his half-crazed mind.

"Can I give you a lift?" the girl asked.

Cary sucked damp air into his aching lungs. For an eternity now he had been tramping on and on, to escape the human bloodhounds who sought to drag him back to justice. Now this girl was leaning from behind the wheel of a mud-splattered roadster saying: "You look awfully tired. Can I give you a lift?"

He mumbled his thanks, slid wearily into the seat beside her. When he relaxed, the vicious throbbing of that half-healed gunshot wound was less agonizing. When he looked into the darkly beautiful face of the girl who had befriended him, some of the maggots of creeping dread stopped their parade through his brain.

"I—I'd been trying," he mumbled, "to reach the next village up the line and find a place to sleep. You going that far?"

She nodded. Her slender hands gripped the wheel firmly as the car labored through ruts that were like black serpents crawling into darkness. "Almost that far. It must be discouraging, trying to get rides on a lonely road like this."

"It is. But I don't dare—" He caught himself in the act of telling her that lonely roads were the only roads he dared travel. His sudden silence made the girl glance abruptly into his face. To kill her quick suspicion he blurted out: "My name's Henry Smith. I'm broke, looking for work."

She said, "Oh!" then lapsed into unnatural silence. Fear came back to Cary's heart warning that she might have recognized him. His picture had been in the papers, surely. That was inevitable. Sensational murder stories made front-page news! But he himself had not seen any papers since that night....

With a sudden grinding jolt the car stopped. Cary's head heaved up; his eyes bulged. Beside him, the dark-eyed girl had gone stiff behind the wheel, her slender hands white and taut on the black rim. In stark terror she was staring ahead through the blurred windshield!

The car's lights made a white aisle in the dark, ate through gloom and picked out an even darker shape that had stepped into the mud of the road—stepped, apparently, from the jungle of underbrush at the roadside. For a breathless interlude of seconds the shape remained motionless, glaring into the car's headlights. Then, with the sudden lunging speed of a cat plunged into the woods!

"Oh—oh, my God!" the girl whispered. "That's *it!* That's the thing from the village! If it comes after us...."

Cary's hands found her shoulders, stilled the trembling of her body. He scowled, tossed his head to clear the black vision from his mind. The thing he had seen was no human shape. Standing there in the road, it had been like some black monk from a forgotten Inquisition chamber, some bloated spectral ghoul spawned in the dark of night. But he stifled the tremor in his voice, demanded harshly: "What are you talking about?"

The girl turned a white, bloodless face. "You—don't understand."

"Understand what?"

"I—I can't tell you! You'll find out soon enough if you stay in this horrible village! There have been murders and—and a hideous thing that prowls in the night...."

She was sincere; yet Cary shrugged. Specters in the night? That was small worry, compared with the black thing that was gnawing even now at his vitals. This girl was afraid of something unreal. He, Cary Booth, feared the clutching fingers of a law that was *real!*

"You think I'm mad," the girl whispered fearfully. "Well, I'm not. It's been going on for—for an eternity. Some horrible thing has descended on the village, to terrify the inhabitants! Innocent people have been slaughtered...."

Cary was not listening. The darkness around him seemed full of creeping black shapes and fearsome fingers that pointed accusingly. Full of Bastone's bloody face that came swimming like a crimson gargoyle through the gloom. How could any man be afraid of ghosts, of faceless black specters, when horribles of his own making were parading through his brain?

DULLY he was aware that the car was in motion. When he heard the girl's voice again, long later, she was saying: "This is as far as I can take you. This is where I live."

Cary peered around. The roadster had quivered to a stop beside a man-high hedge that ran on into darkness. A gravel driveway angled to the left, toward a huge white house that loomed against crowding pine-woods. Windows glowed palely, upstairs and down. A light gleamed on the wide veranda.

"The village is a quarter-mile farther on," the girl said. "And—" She stiffened, stopped talking. Approaching feet made a crunching sound in gravel and a tall straight shape came through the hedge-opening. The girl exhaled slowly, seemed relieved as the approaching shape proved to be a well-dressed young man with dark hair, dark staring eyes.

"Is that you, Irma?"

The girl said quickly: "Yes. Yes, John." She frowned into the man's face as he put a foot on the running-board and peered into the car. "John, this is Mr. Henry Smith." She turned impulsively to Cary. "My brother, John Sibley. I gave Mr. Smith a lift, John. I'd ask him to stay the night, but I don't think father would like it. Do you?"

"I'm sure he wouldn't."

Cary opened the car door. "That's quite all right. If there's an inn—"

"Yes, there's an inn." John Sibley hooked his mouth into a scowling crescent, narrowed his dark eyes. "But if I were you, I'd think twice before—" He stopped. Behind him the front door of the big house had opened noisily and a tall dark figure was standing motionless on the veranda, glaring. A harsh voice bellowed: "John! Irma! What are you doing out there at this time of night?"

The girl sighed, put a hand on Cary Booth's arm. "You'll have to go. Father throws a fit when he finds us talking to strangers. It's because of—of what's been going on in the village. I'm sorry." She turned her face toward him, and Cary saw the hurt look that had come suddenly into her dark eyes. "But John is right. *Don't go to the inn, Mr. Smith.*"

She wanted to say something else. Cary was sure of it. When he looked back after walking a hundred yards down the rutted road, the car was moving slowly into the drive, and that other shape, glaring accusingly, was still tall and gaunt in the glow of the veranda light.

He, Cary Booth, was evidently not the only person who lived in shadow. Something in Irma Sibley's deep, dark eyes....

The sign, leering down like a face with broken teeth, said *Red Hand Inn*. With misgiving in his heart, Cary peered again around the abandoned village square. The houses all were dark; there was no other place to go. He climbed the steps, put out a groping hand and let the iron knocker thud into its slot. The warning words of John Sibley echoed in his mind.

The door creaked open. Watery eyes, sunk deep in the unclean flesh of a woman's face, glared through gloom. Fat and slovenly, the woman crowded the doorway with her enormous bulk. "What is it you want? A room?"

"Yes." Cary's reply came falteringly. "Yes. A room for the night."

"Come in then. It's late but—well, come in." The woman stepped back. With Cary following, she waddled, wheezing in her throat, down a dimly lighted corridor into a musty, sour-smelling room that was obviously a sitting-room. Two others were in the room.

The place was old. Painted walls were cracked so badly that they bore strange designs, crooked faces that leered ominously as Cary advanced. "You ain't told me your name," the woman said.

"It's Smith. Henry Smith."

"Well, I'm Mariah Gravlin and this here is my husband, Abel. The boy's our son, Saul." She swung toward a teenaged youth who swayed slowly back and forth, like a human clock-pendulum, in a high-backed rocker. "Can't you say hello to the gentleman, Saul?"

The boy made a grunting sound in his throat and Cary stared, realized that the son of Mariah and Abel Gravlin was a half wit. The thought sent a shudder through him. A strange house, this into which he had wandered! But a good house, for him. The police....

Abel Gravlin's keen eyes swept Cary from head to foot, missed nothing. Like a gnome in some dark grotto, he sat hunched in his chair and the chair was bigger than he, despite the deformity that made a camel-hump of his bent back.

Abel Gravlin was no moron. In a slow, deliberate voice he said: "This is a strange hour to be seeking shelter."

"I've come a long way."

"Yes, I can see that." Those unblinking eyes bored holes in Cary's soul.

With a sudden tremor Cary stepped back, looked at the old woman. "I—I'm very tired. Will you show me my room?"

Mariah Gravlin shrugged her flabby shoulders. "Saul. Show the gentleman a room upstairs."

The moron son scuffed forward like a ventriloquist's dummy.

His hand made a sucking sound on the staircase railing as he ascended. Cary followed.

AT the top the boy stopped, held a match to a gas-jet that protruded like a gnarled human hand, long dead, from the scarred wall. Methodically he scuffed along the hall, stopped before a closed door and fumbled a ring of keys out of his pocket.

"Am I the only guest staying here tonight?" Cary asked stiffly.

"Nope." Again the boy struck a match, this time carried the flame over the threshold and used it to ignite a jet in the room beyond. He turned, put a hand on the doorknob. "If you want anythin', come to the head of the stairs and holler. I'll be around most all night."

The door clicked shut. Cary Booth exhaled slowly and looked around him.

It was a small room. A frayed carpet covered part of the painted floor, and the walls were yellow, scarred with age. But it was a room and afforded privacy. And Cary Booth was tired.

The creeping things in his soul had eaten away his resistance; miles and miles of weary tramping had added to his exhaustion. The wound in his side was beginning to throb again.

The wound would be festered now. But there was water in a basin on the wooden washstand. Wearily, Cary sat on the bed, stripped off shirt and undershirt and bared the inflamed flesh. Beyond the gas-jet, Bastone's death-head took form and leered at him in silent triumph.

Bastone! Cary Booth thought suddenly of the girl in the roadster. Madge, his sister, had been like her. Madge had been sweet and lovely until Bastone had put his vile hands on her, defiling her. But Madge was changed. That dead, dull look of black shame in her eyes....

And Bastone was in hell, sent there by Cary Booth's clenched fists! The night Madge had come home weeping and sobbing, Cary Booth had gone mad, gone to find Bastone. And the man had denied nothing, had stood there in the sitting-room of his luxurious apartment and sneered indifferently: "Well, what of it, Booth? Your sister isn't a child! Don't be a damned fool!"

Then... those two fists had battered Bastone's sneering face to pulp, had slammed his tall thin body all over the apartment, following him as he ran screaming from room to room. His screams had aroused the house, brought police and gaping civilians to the scene. But the police had come too late, had arrived only to find Bastone bleeding and battered in a contorted heap on the floor.

And Cary Booth had escaped! Had raced blindly down the hall to a window that overlooked the courtyard. Police bullets had shrieked after him, one of them searing his side. But he had escaped. And now, days later....

He stared at the shadowy face that leered out at him. And then, with a sudden suck of breath, Cary Booth sat rigid, listening.

The sound was a fugitive *slap, slap* of naked feet prowling along the corridor outside, beyond the door that Saul Gravlin had drawn shut. Slowly it came nearer. For an instant the feet seemed to hesitate as they came opposite the door; then they continued their sinister parade.

With a swift, silent leap, Cary was off the bed, standing flat against the closed barrier. His hand sought the knob, turned it soundlessly. A cold, unreasoning fear was in his heart.

Then he saw, and his eyes bulged in their dark sockets. Less than ten paces from him, a tall naked shape moved in the yellow gaslight that blurred the corridor. Like a corpse risen from the dead, the creature paced slowly forward, walking stiffly on legs that seemed weighted.

The shape was a man... a large man, stark naked, with bloated arms....

Rigid as the doorframe to which he clung, Cary stood watching, fearful lest the thumping of his heart should reach the naked one's ears and cause the man to turn. But the prowler did not stop. With the same mechanical stride he continued down the corridor and became a blurred shape in shadows before ceasing his advance. Then, as if bewildered, he turned from one door to another, finally thrusting one of them open and vanishing across the dark threshold.

The door closed. Cary Booth stared into an empty corridor. The sound of a watch ticking—a watch in his own trousers pocket—was the only alien noise in the tomblike silence of the inn. Then, from the far side of the door that had just clicked shut, came a sound that jarred its fearsome way into his soul!

A woman—screaming! Blood rushed to Cary's head and surged at his wire-tight nerve centers as the shrill cry of agony tocsined through silence. Stark terror was in it, and fear beyond measurement. In wailing waves of bloodcurdling horror it surged along the corridor, rocking him backward as if a crimson fist had crashed into him.

Then he was snarling forward, lurching down the hall toward the door where that evil naked shape had vanished!

THE door jarred open, crashed against the inner wall as Cary's lunging body made savage contact. Sucking breath, he reeled across the black threshold, stumbled forward with both hands outthrust. Something soft, something flabby and ponderous, made contact with his outflung palms and reeled drunkenly away.

His feet slithered beneath him as they encountered a pool of wet slime. He went down, sprawled headlong. A stench of blood filled his throat and gagged him. Agony stabbed his side as hot fluid burned the inflamed flesh of his old wound.

Frantically he pushed himself up, stood swaying. The room was dark as the inside of a death-vault. When he struck a match, the sputtering light revealed just enough to send him stumbling backward, eyes wide with sudden dread.

Facing him, propped against the room's rear wall, stood the same naked shape that had crept along the corridor outside. More than ever the man resembled a resurrected corpse. But something marred the whiteness of his flesh now. The splayed fingers of his hands dripped carmine, his mouth and face were smeared with blood. Dully he returned Cary's stare, made no move to advance.

The match in Cary's hand burned low, reached a gas-jet just in time. Voices, footsteps, were audible on the staircase that led from the lower floor. Slowly, Cary moved forward. Then he stiffened.

With a low moan the naked shape swayed toward him, sagged to the floor as if life had suddenly ebbed out of it!

Cary shuddered, went to his knees and put trembling hands on the man's twitching body. The body was bloated now, swollen through chest and shoulders to half again its normal size. The hands were opening and closing like hungry crabs. The man's lips drooled blood.

Beyond that moaning shape a door hung open—a door that led, apparently, to an adjoining chamber.

Cary's hands found a grip on the bloated body, lost the grip when the body was racked suddenly with violent convulsions. Across the threshold behind him came the slovenly, gasping figure of Mariah Gravlin, and other occupants of the inn crowded in to stand staring.

A woman screamed hysterically. Abel Gravlin limped forward, glared down with enormous eyes. Mariah looked into the naked man's face and sucked breath until her flabby chest was a bulging double-topped mountain.

"So it's him, is it? Him, with blood all over him! Blood on his mouth!" She swung viciously on her husband. "That's what I always said, isn't it? Didn't I always say there was somethin' queer about him? He ain't human! He's one of them there vampires you hear tell about!"

Blood... on his mouth. Cary Booth shuddered, stared down at the sticky stuff on his own hands, his own half-naked body. The woman was mad, of course! Her hideous insinuations could not be true! And yet....

He had no time to think. Mariah Gravlin ceased glaring into the man's crimson face and screamed hoarsely: "Well, what are you all standin' around for? It's blood, isn't it? Why'n't you find out *whose blood it is?*"

It was a gibbering, muttering line of scarecrows that filed out of the horror-room and marched down the corridor behind the leadership of the innkeeper's wife. Cary Booth, staring after them, blurted out hoarsely: "But you can't leave him here! He's not dead—"

"He's a vampire, that's what he is!" the woman shrilled. "Leave him be!"

CARY stooped, raised the naked form in his arms and carried it to the bed. Bending over it, he narrowed his eyes and examined the man, studied those wide orbs and the blood-filled mouth. In college, Cary Booth had studied medicine....

He stepped back, his brain working dully in an effort to fit together the pieces of the crimson puzzle. Wrinkles furrowed his forehead as he stared around the room.

The chamber had two doors. Through one of them, this strange naked shape had entered from the corridor after hesitating out there, apparently unsure of which door to select. Then he had paced over the threshold into this chamber of darkness, and a moment later a woman had screamed in soul-retching agony.

The second door, at the deep end of the chamber, hung open. Cary strode over the sill, struck a match.

He shrank back, staring in horror. The match quivered in his fingers and made a thin yellow zigzag to the floor. Seconds passed before he found strength enough to light a gas-jet.

The blood in his rigid body had thinned to water. Slowly, he stepped forward.

The room had one occupant—a woman. Naked as the strange creature in the adjoining chamber, she hung head downward from the center of the ceiling, her butchered body suspended from what had been a ponderous gas-fixture.

She was a large, heavy-breasted woman of questionable age. Like a side of beef in a slaughterhouse, she dangled in mid-air, her artificially blonde hair scraping the floor.

Blood had ceased to flow but had not yet begun to coagulate. It puddled around her throat, her mouth, and the floor beneath her hanging head.

And there was something else that dragged Cary Booth forward, made him fight back a wave of horror and bend to look closer. From the woman's left breast hung a ragged square of paper, blood-smeared and sinister, pinned there by a gleaming needle that pierced her heart. Words glared back into Cary's wide eyes. Words printed blackly but glowing now through a blood-smear that made them all but illegible.

He heard a scuffing of feet on the threshold behind him but did not turn. Slowly he made out the crudely lettered message, and was reading it in terrible fascination when other denizens of the inn crowded around him.

The words on that stained square of paper were significant, replete with red evil. They said hideously: *"It is written that the dead shall return. Take warning, ye who walk in life! This is a house of shadows where the living may not safely abide!"*

Behind Cary a woman screamed hysterically and slumped to the blood-wet floor. But Cary did not turn. Still staring at the crimson message, he took note grimly, through the haze of terror that threatened to engulf him, of the strange preciseness of the words. And recalled dully how Abel Gravlin had addressed him, downstairs in the sitting-room, in the same careful choice of syllables.

But there was something else. In the throat of the butchered woman before him gaped a jagged, carmine hole—and Mariah Gravlin was croaking gutturally: "Look at her! It was vampire's teeth that done that to her neck! Ain't I always said as how that fiend in the next room had teeth that wasn't human? Go look at them! They're long and sharp and—"

Cary straightened, turned slowly to stare into the terrified faces around him. His gaze focused dully on the proprietor.

"You'd better call the police."

The answer came not from Abel Gravlin but from somewhere beyond the confines of the room itself—from somewhere in the black, crawling shadows of the corridor outside. Beginning in a slow whisper, the sound increased in volume until it was a hoarse bubbling cacophony of guttural laughter, laughter that rolled like a living entity into the room where the occupants of the house stood.

Then it ceased, but not before it had drained the color from the face of every person present and left a winding-sheet of cold nameless dread through which no person dared speak!

CHAPTER TWO

THE FACE OF THE GHOUL

IN THE sitting-room of the Red Hand Inn, a muttering, whispering group of terror-stricken people sat waiting.

After that hideous outburst of mirth in the upstairs corridor, Abel Gravlin had been the first to lurch from the death-room. Cary Booth had been on his heels, had overtaken him and passed him to lead a frenzied search for the creator of the hellish laughter. But the search had revealed nothing. "You had better call the police," Cary said again.

Abel Gravlin's eyes were small black beetles in a gray face. "That is impossible. There are but two telephones in the village. One is in the General Store, whose owner is spending the night with friends in Norton. The other phone—" He made fists of his gnarled hands and let his hollow voice sink to a deep-throated rasp— "is in the home of Lannon Sibley; he does not welcome intruders!"

Cary thought of the girl who had given him a lift, and of the tall, domineering man who had bellowed from the veranda of the big house on the outskirts of the village. He wanted suddenly to ask questions about Lannon Sibley. Obviously the villagers were in awe of the man and feared him. But why?

"I suggest," Gravlin said precisely, "that we all return to our rooms. We are as safe in our individual rooms, behind locked doors, as we are here."

His unlovely wife nodded her head, pushed thick fingers through her mop of hair. Saul, the moron son, sat like a discarded puppet on the bare floor, his back against the rungs of a vacant rocker. Obviously the events of the night had made no impression on his feeble brain.

The other occupants of the room were a strange lot. One, a dumpy, balloon-bodied man who called himself Quentin Planchard, had been acting the part of an amateur detective, thinking up idiotic questions and demanding answers. According to his own statement, he had come to Troville for a rest.

That was perhaps a lie. According to Miss Hattie Benson, the over-dressed maiden lady who sat wringing her hands in near hysteria, the man had come to Troville for the concealed purpose of buying property—if he could do so cheaply. In a few months a new state road would pass through the village; property would increase in value. And Quentin Planchard possessed a mind far shrewder than his bilious facial expression indicated.

On the side, to Cary alone, the old maid had whispered other information. Did he know, perhaps, that Abel Gravlin was not the inn's original owner? That Gravlin had come to Troville only a few years ago, after resigning as professor of chemistry in a nearby State College? It night be well to keep that information in mind! Abel Gravlin had plunged into a most unfortunate marriage while still a youth in college. The marriage had spawned a moron son. For years, Gravlin had lived in shame and then, in despair, had ceased fighting such overwhelming odds, resigned his position, and sought seclusion in Troville.

A strange group! And now, muttering and mumbling among themselves, they were parading from the room, ascending the staircase to the floor above. Quietly, Cary Booth turned to Mariah Gravlin.

"The man in that room upstairs, the man you think is a vampire, needs attention or he may die. I've studied to be a doctor. Will you help me?"

"It'd be better if he does die!"

"But he may be able to tell us—"

The woman shrugged, followed Cary upstairs and into the gas-lit chamber where that naked shape lay sprawled on the bed. A new thought darkened Cary's eyes then. Mariah Gravlin, in leading the search for the vampire's victim, had deliberately ignored the door which even now hung open at the far end of the chamber. Surely the woman had seen that door and realized the significance of its being open. Yet....

"There's a medicine cabinet in the bathroom," Mariah rasped, "if you want to use it." Savagely she glared at the naked thing on the bed, and was still glaring as Cary strode down the hall.

Returning, he bent above the bed and swabbed blood from the bloated shape that lay there, but the man either would not or could not regain consciousness. Moans came hollowly from the twisted lips; the glassy eyes twitched; but life refused to flow back into that rigid body.

"His name's Redfern," the woman said nasally. "He's been here for most three weeks and sick all the time. That is, he's been actin' sick, but I'm keepin' my thoughts to myself!"

"Is this his room?"

"No, it ain't. His room's acrost the hall."

Cary paced across the hall and put a hand on the doorknob. The door was unlocked. Inside, a light burned low and the bed was a crumpled, bloodstained shambles. Scowling, Cary returned to the stricken man and worked over him.

A vampire? Such thoughts were madness! And yet—the door leading to the adjoining chamber was open, and in that chamber hung a woman whose throat....

Cary straightened, stared into the defiant face of Mariah Gravlin and admitted defeat. "He's in a coma. In the morning you'd better call a doctor."

Then he walked slowly down the hall and into his own room, closing the door.

BUT there was no door that he could close on his thoughts, and they were black slugs crawling in fearsome procession through his brain. The excruciating pain was back in his side, revived by his exertions of the past hour. Sick in mind and body, he flung himself on the bed, lay in a sprawled heap and stared blankly up at the scarred ceiling.

A small thin voice, strangely like the dying voice of Bastone, whispered inside him, driving its evil message through his dulled nerves. The horror of this night had only begun. This was penance for the sin of taking another man's life. This hell had been prepared for his benefit.

The room was deathly still; the house that nurtured it was a vault of ominous silence, silence that he knew to be peopled with crawling shapes of horror which before long would leave their hidden retreats and prowl on evil missions.

Then the silence was broken. Furtive feet made a soft *shf, shf, shf* in the corridor beyond the door of the room. That door was closed, not locked. Cary lay rigid, waiting....

His racked body refused to move, would not lurch erect. Outside the door the approaching *shf, shf* of ominous footsteps came to a slow halt. The knob turned slowly, so slowly that it seemed not to move at all. Soundlessly the door inched inward... and Cary watched with eyes that refused to close, eyes bulging like frosted glass marbles from his rigid head.

The door did not open wide. Through the narrow aperture came black groping fingers, fingers that belonged to no human hand but to a black ghoul from some dark temple of unholy silence! Like ebony night-crawlers, they slid around the edge of the door and fastened on the key that protruded from the inside.

Then they slithered silently from sight, gripping the key in their black embrace.

Before Cary's blurred brain leaped to a realization of the black-handed one's intent, the key made a scraping sound in the lock, on the outside. The lock clicked dully, imprisoning him!

Cary Booth sat motionless, victim of a nameless dread that made of his aching body a thing of wood, powerless to move. He was a prisoner, held captive in a room that had only one narrow window—a window that overlooked a thirty-foot drop into darkness! And there had been no retreating echo of footsteps in the silence of the corridor. The owner of those hideous black fingers had not stolen away but was still waiting, outside!

The gas-jet was still sputtering and for that Cary was vibrant with gratitude. He forced himself off the bed, made his quivering body stand erect. Then in the act of moving forward he froze stiff again, widened his glazed eyes at a thin, tenuous serpent-shape

Inn of the Shadow-Creatures 69

that curled beneath the door and writhed toward him.

He had only a moment in which to stare. With a sudden sputtering sound, the gas-jet in the wall beside him burned low; its flame became a sickly yellow thing flickering feebly and clinging to the jet's nostril as if fighting against black fingers that sought to push it away. With a sucking hiss the yellow flame expired; the room was in darkness!

But still that white, smoky snake curled beneath the door and invaded the chamber, twining forward and losing shape as it prowled toward Cary's fear-racked form. With it came an odor of bitter almonds, faint but growing more definite. Cary stumbled back, sobbing. Bitter almonds could mean only one thing! The invader was poison gas!

Its stench seared his throat as he sucked breath. In a thick white cloud the gas swirled toward him, licked at his legs, rose slowly higher and clung to his body despite his stumbling efforts to avoid it. Like a clawing, sharp-nailed hand, it raked his throat, stabbed into his nostrils and gagged him, made him retch, cough explosively. His throat afire, blind terror took possession of his lurching body. Numbness crept into him.

With the numbness came a face, a leering death's-head born out of his distorted brain. Bastone's face, chortling words of triumphant glee in the darkness.

Cary lurched backward, spun on the balls of his feet and heaved himself at the room's single window. His hands clawed the frame, fingernails scratching at cracked paint. But the window was old, swollen by recent rains. It stuck.

He swayed around, made a hoarse sobbing noise in his tortured throat as he ploughed forward. Bastone's face was still leering, still grinning. The face did things to Cary Booth's soul, filled him with screaming rage that welled in a wave of lurid sound from his lips. His hands closed, balled into fists, lashed out.

NOTHING was there to meet the sweep of his arms. Nothing but darkness and a grim gray serpent coiling sinuously through the room, writhing about him, sucking him into its embrace.

Madness seized him then and flowed over him in a black,

blinding wave that rushed through the pores of his body, found its way into the bubbling blood of his heart. Out there in the hall, some black-handed fiend of hell was crouching, waiting in gleeful triumph for the poison gas to take effect... some monster of the nethermost torment-temples of a lurid hell, with a scheming, diabolical brain, a brain that had missed nothing, that had somehow contrived even to plunge the death-chamber into darkness, that the horror might be complete! Black hands... and a black face grinning....

Cary's lunging body crashed against a chair, swayed drunkenly. He retched like a man sick with liquor, fell sideways across the bed and lay there groaning. Instinct shrieked at him to get up again, made him drag his agony-racked body erect. His hands found the wooden rungs of the chair, raised it high. Like a drunken man he staggered to the door.

After that, his actions were mechanical. A guttural gas-choked voice within him growled the word *fight*, bellowed at him to stay on his feet! Unintelligible sounds groaned from his parched lips. The chair in his hands made crashing contact with the door, rose and fell like a sledge in the hands of a lazy blacksmith.

The chair splintered, broke, and still he swung it. Breath choked in his throat; cold sweat oozed from the tight flesh of his forehead and blinded him, coursed down his twitching face and mingled with the scarlet foam that flecked his drooling mouth. The door shivered, groaned on protesting hinges. Then it yielded.

It clattered outward with a splintering crash, lock and hinges broken by the chair's assault. The frantic heave that smashed it sent Cary headlong over the threshold, drove him like a gasping scarecrow across the corridor. The wall stopped him, thudded against his contorted body. He lurched clear and stood like a dynamited building ready to crash.

He did not fall. Cool damp air whined into his lungs. Swaying with both hands outflung, he regained balance, flung his head up to kill the sickness within him.

His bulging eyes stared through the corridor's gloom. His body stiffened with a convulsive jerk. A shriek rose in his throat and died there against lips too numb to spill it forth.

The corridor was an aisle of darkness. Gas-flames no longer flickered to relieve the ebony winding-sheet. But there was something else, something that glowed in the gloom like a white, fleshless skull!

It was a face, looming above a black, shapeless torso that moved with the gliding ease of a monstrous slug. And this time it was not Bastone's face, not a creation of Cary Booth's tortured nerves—but real! A countenance of living death, dragged from some violated grave!

Then the spectral ghoul was gone, gone with fantastic abruptness as if a cloud of black vapor had suddenly engulfed it. Cary lurched forward, blind with a mad desire to tear it to shreds, mutilate it and shriek with insane triumph while the thing screamed for mercy!

A dozen staggering strides he took before his madness died in a black wave of sickness. Agony welled through his tortured body, clutched at him like a giant octopus with countless clawing arms. He stumbled, pitched sideways against the wall and clung there, fighting the shroud of darkness that rushed over him. His lungs were bursting, his mouth a bottomless pit of devouring flame. The old bullet wound in his side was open again, scalding his leg with hot blood.

A long, shuddering moan crawled from his burning throat as he fell. The moan was answered—answered by a shrill, enduring cry of stark terror, emanating from a room at the end of the corridor. For an eternity the shriek rang in his ears, eating its vibrant way into his numbed brain... as if some fiend of hell were turning the handle of a death-siren, calling another victim to a bloody end.

Again the victim was a woman. That shrieking voice of terror....

Cary Booth did not hear its gurgling diminuendo, did not know when the voice at last ceased screaming. In a dark hell-world of his own, he lay sprawled on the floor, unconscious.

HE opened his eyes to look into the ugly, twisted face of the inn's hunchbacked proprietor, and Abel Gravlin's dark orbs glared back at him unblinkingly, filled with wriggling worms of black hate.

Beyond the innkeeper's unlovely face, other faces loomed in the ocher light of the sitting-room.

Mariah Gravlin was there, and the halfwit Saul. Quentin Planchard, the real-estate man, sat stiffly in a broken-backed rocker. One of the Benson sisters was slumped in a musty over-stuffed chair, her face lowered in spread-fingered hands, ghastly sobs spurting from her lips.

Terror was in Cary's soul and the terror lingered a long while before abandoning its sucking grip. He stared, failed at first to realize where he was or to remember what had happened. Then his roving gaze encountered a silent shape that lay within ten feet of him, and he surged forward in his chair, a shriek welling in his throat.

Wire-tight ropes yanked his contorted body back again, sent new agony through his arms and legs. Bewildered, he gaped down. His arms and legs were bound. His trembling body, clotted with blood, was lashed to the chair in which he sat!

Understanding came to him slowly. The blood was his own. Upstairs in the hall he had pitched unconscious, lain there in a gathering scarlet pool that spilled from the wound in his side....

But the blood on that other shape was not his! Wide-eyed, he fought back the sickness that gurgled into his throat. This was the woman who had screamed, whose screams had tocsined in his ears as he lost consciousness. Abel Gravlin and the others had spread her naked, mutilated body on the divan here.

She was the woman who had threatened to leave at daybreak. The woman who called herself Hattie Benson. But she would not leave now—not of her own volition. When she went, it would be in an oblong box, and her body would be wrapped in a grim winding-sheet, so that the horror of her death-agonies could not appall the men who carried her!

With an effort Cary wrenched his gaze away, stared again into the immobile mask of Abel Gravlin's frog-face. Gravlin was saying, not to him but to the assembled guests: "It would be best for all of you to return to your rooms. There is nothing more to fear, now that we have captured the killer. My wife and I will keep him here until daylight, when it will be possible to call the police

Inn of the Shadow-Creatures

and have them come for him!"

Cary's eyes bulged, showed white. "Good God! You don't think that I—that I—" Terror leaped inside him; his blood-drenched hands fought against wet ropes as he strained forward. "No! No! I didn't do it! You've made a mistake!"

Gravlin ignored him, said again to the anxious-eyed guests: "Go to your rooms and remain there."

They obeyed him. Whispering among themselves, they filed from the room. Only one person, Quentin Planchard, turned to look back at the bound prisoner, and Cary Booth thought for a mad moment that those boring eyes were alive with furtive triumph. Then the eyes were gone and Abel Gravlin was saying nasally: "If you make even the slightest attempt to escape, I shall be forced to use this!"

His gnarled hands closed over an iron poker. "Do you understand?"

"I tell you you're mad!" Cary shrieked. "Raving mad! I'm not responsible for what happened to Miss Benson! The fiend who killed her tried to kill me, too!"

"Really?" The innkeeper's voice was syrupy sweet with sarcasm. "Then perhaps you know the fiend's identity?"

"No! But I saw his face. I saw a face that—" Cary caught himself, clamped his lips on the words and knew that talking would get him nowhere. These people were right; circumstantial evidence was piled mountain-high against him.

They had heard the Benson woman's terror-shrieks. Investigating, they had found her dead, murdered. Then, not twenty feet from the door of the death-room they had discovered his own unconscious body sprawled in the corridor, in a lake of fresh blood. Blood on his hands, on his face, on his lips!

That blood was his own! But he could not tell them that! He could not show them the wound in his side and—and blurt out the truth. They would know him then for the murderer of Bastone, the killer whom the police were even now looking for! Such a move would be madness, would brand him with guilt, would make Abel Gravlin even more certain that he had slaughtered the Benson woman!

Despairingly he slumped in his chair, stared out of gas-burned eyes. This was the end. This was penance for taking a human life. It mattered not that the life he took had been a vile thing, unfit to exist. A life was a life. And a relentless god of judgment was demanding his in return for Bastone's....

THE room was silent—as silent, Cary thought, as the black vault which would soon contain his own tortured body. Death would be merciful now. Bastone's face would no longer leer.

Dull resignation gripped him. Terror died within him and a numbness chilled him as he gazed dully at Abel Gravlin, at Mariah, at their son Saul who was again swaying back and forth, back and forth like a human pendulum, in a rocker that creaked dismally with every slow move.

The chair-creaks counted seconds, eternities. Abel Gravlin stood up, glared at his wife. "I am going upstairs to make certain that everything is well. While I'm gone, you might make coffee. Saul can watch this wretch."

He limped slowly up the stairs. The woman peered at her moron son and said raspingly: "You hear? You are to stand guard. If this beast tries to escape, yell so we can hear!"

Cary peered at the son, and he and Saul were alone in the room. The halfwit had stopped rocking, was indifferently making shadow-shapes with his fingers and moving his hands against the light to give the shadows life on the floor. The slow scuff of Mariah's receding footsteps died to silence. Cary leaned forward, recognizing an opportunity for escape! The son of Abel and Mariah Gravlin was a halfwit. Perhaps....

"Listen, Saul." Cary's voice was a cracked whisper, pitched low. "Listen. You know I didn't kill that woman. *Don't* you?"

The boy raised an expressionless face.

"Listen." Cary's bloody hands worked feverishly at the ropes that bound them. Behind his back, their frantic movements were hidden from the moron's dull gaze. "We're friends. If you were in trouble, I'd help *you* out. Will you help me?"

"No." The boy shook his head, uninterested, and again made shadow-shapes with his fingers. "Nope. I won't."

Inn of the Shadow-Creatures 75

Blood rushed to Cary's face, colored the sucked-in flesh of his gaunt cheeks. It was now or never! There would never be another chance! "You're mad!" he hissed. "Do you know what will happen to you if they put me to death?" His writhing hands, lubricated by warm blood, slipped free of their bonds; one of them slid furtively into a back-pocket of his trousers and closed over a pen-knife that Abel Gravlin, thank God, had not seen fit to remove. "If I die, I'll come back from the darkness beyond the grave and destroy you! Ever hear of *vampires?*"

No trace of terror showed in the boy's face. He stared; that was all. A sneer curled his thin lips and he shrugged his shoulders. "Yeah, I've heard my maw tell about 'em. What of it?"

Cary lunged forward with a hoarse intake of breath. The knife in his hand swept down, slashed the ropes that bound his ankles. Without straightening, he hurtled from the chair, hurled the gaping half wit aside with a flailing sweep of one arm. Then he was out of the room, racing blindly to freedom!

Behind him the moron's shrill voice shrieked out: "Maw! *Maw!* He's got away! *Maw!*—" Heavy blundering feet pounded the floor and a woman's voice rasped in coarse crescendo. Other feet, belonging to Abel Gravlin, thundered on the staircase from the floor above.

But Cary's out-thrust hand slapped the front door, yanked the bolt and clawed the barrier open. The gaping aperture vomited his staggering body into cool darkness. He was out! Outside! A hoarse cry spewed from his lips and his tortured heart sang a delirious chant of triumph. Drunkenly he lurched down the veranda steps and raced into the night.

CHAPTER THREE
BLACK CLAWS

BUT ESCAPE was not to be so easy. Before Cary Booth had crossed the village square, dark shapes were lurching through shadows behind him; shrill voices bellowed a raucous clamor. The beam of a powerful searchlight swept through murk and found his stumbling form.

A rifle belched, sent mad echoes racing across the square. Something made a whistling sound within inches of Cary's face. He lunged sideways, escaped the betraying beam of light, raced again.

His stumbling feet found the road along which he had traveled into Troville's realm of horror, the road that led past the big white home of Lannon Sibley. Breath sobbed from his gas-burned lungs as he ran. Behind him the dark shapes in the square had multiplied; men's voices spewed forth a wolf-pack howl.

Then another sound wailed against Cary's eardrums, spiked his laboring heart with cold dread and watered the blood in his lurching legs. Dogs! Hound-dogs, baying eerily through the night as they picked up his trail!

The sound wailed after him, trailed him relentlessly as he raced on. Frantically he tried to smother his line of flight, stumbled from the road into deep grass, splashed through a narrow ditch that might kill the scent of his body. But the attempt was futile. His flesh reeked with a stench of hot blood, and that betraying stench was as easy to follow as a phosphorescent fire-streak in the dark!

Terror had him in its savage grip before the white bulk of

Lannon Sibley's home loomed in gloom ahead. Terror made him race from the road-shoulder and lurch blindly across-lots toward that looming bulk. Behind him, pursuing hounds filled the night with mad din.

Desperate hope flamed now in Cary's heart. This house before him—a girl lived there! A girl with lovely dark eyes and compassion in her heart! She had befriended him once. Perhaps....

Hope gave him strength to claw his way through the man-high hedge and stumble across the lawn beyond. The house loomed above him, its owlish windows leering down in darkness. Sobbing, he dragged himself along the wall, found a door at the rear. The door was locked.

But there was something else—a black bulkhead that yielded to the frantic tug of his fingers. Rasping open, the thing revealed stone steps angling downward into the gloom of a cellar. The bulkhead thudded shut above Cary's hunched shoulders, smothering the eerie ululation that spilled from the slavering tongues of hungry hounds.

Slowly, fearfully, he prowled into the vault of darkness beneath Lannon Sibley's huge dwelling.

The cellar was enormous, a subterranean domain of darkness filled with bulging black shapes. Cary's distorted mind transformed the shapes into lurking monsters, and he cringed from them. Pawing his way forward, he shuddered when his hands made contact with the chill wall of a dead furnace. His stumbling feet kicked a coal-scuttle, sent the thing clanging across the floor with a din that would have aroused the dead.

When he stopped, stood motionless, hounds were baying hungrily outside the house and the ceiling above him creaked ominously as slow-moving feet paced across a floor....

A door inched open at the head of a flight of wooden stairs. Light streaked downward, stabbing the cellar's gloom. The stairs groaned protestingly under the pressure of descending feet.

Cary stared wide-eyed, shrank back against the wall of the furnace and stood rigid. Down the shaft of white light, as if born in it and spawned by it, came a menacing black shape, thin and gaunt. The light made a monstrous specter of it, hurling its shadow in gigantic relief across the cellar floor. Slowly, step by step, the intruder descended....

Then a sob choked on Cary's lips; he wanted suddenly to hurl out a shriek of insane laughter. The thing was human! It was no dark demon out of hell; it had familiar features and was saying in an anxious, fearful voice: "Who's there?"

The intruder was John Sibley. John—the dark-eyed, slightly dissipated looking young man who had seen fit, long ago, to warn Cary Booth against spending the night at the Red Hand Inn!

IN his relief, Cary allowed his rigid body to relax. Even that slight movement attracted the other man's attention. Halting with a jerk, Sibley stared through darkness, jerked up a rigid hand that held a revolver. Raspingly he flung out: "Come out of there, you! I'll shoot!"

Cary had no choice. Silently he stepped forward, moved into the shaft of light from the open door above. Hope died in his breast. He could expect no help here. The face of John Sibley was an angry mask; he glared sullenly, snapped out: "What's the meaning of this?"

"I'm hiding from a pack of bloodthirsty men and dogs. Listen!"

He whipped up his arm, pointed. Sibley sucked breath and said abruptly: "Good God!"

"They think I'm responsible for the horrors that occurred at the inn tonight." Cary lurched forward, clawed the other man's arm. "So help me God, I'm as innocent as you are, Sibley! I've walked in hell tonight, but it wasn't a hell of my own making. I swear it!"

Sibley jerked back, stared at him. The man's eyes were narrowed, dark with suspicion; they bored holes in Cary's gaunt face, seeking truth. Like a doomed wretch on the scaffold, Cary awaited the verdict, knew that he had no strength left to fight if the verdict went against him.

Then Sibley's eyes softened; he lowered the gun in his fist and moved his head up and down slowly. "I know what the villagers are like," he said quietly. "Being a son of Lannon Sibley, I've taken plenty of abuse from them myself. They're savage beasts, the whole lot of them. They hate my father, hate me because I'm his son." His mouth tightened as if the words had an acid taste. Then: "Come. You can't hide here. Come upstairs. Irma and I will...."

Cary followed him like a man suddenly drawn from the flames of hell and granted a pardon.

At the top of the stairs John Sibley clicked the cellar light out, turned left and paced through a broad kitchen. He stopped, stood scowling as alien sounds ate through the walls and disturbed the stillness of the house. Men and dogs were out there in darkness, clamoring for blood, for Cary Booth's lifeblood!

"Savage beasts, the lot of them!" Sibley snarled. "By God, I'd hide even a bloody murderer from them if I had the chance, and you're not a murderer." He peered into Cary's face, nodded slowly. "No, you're not. I'm no fool!"

He strode into a narrow hall, thrust open a door. "You can hide in here. They won't search the house; they won't dare. They think my father's a madman." He laughed mirthlessly, hunched his lean shoulders. "Maybe they're right about that. Anyway, it's a good thing for you they think so. I'll tell Irma you're here, and when the filthy beasts have gone away I'll take you out of here in my car, to be sure you get safely away."

He snapped a light-switch, turned and strode away. Slowly, Cary paced into the room and drew the door shut. It was a den, small, musty, with a blackened fireplace and row upon row of somber shelves lined with books. He slumped in a worn leather chair, pushed himself erect again and paced the floor. Even here in the bowels of the house the shrill baying of the hounds was audible, seeping in like an unceasing ghost-voice!

He shuddered, paced back and forth across the shadowed room in a desperate effort to keep his nerves together. Hysteria was a leering shape that dogged his steps, with writhing hands outflung to seize him. If he let go....

Behind him the door creaked; he whirled about, heart thumping with new terror. The terror was slow in dying. The face he looked into was stern, not soft with compassion as he had frantically hoped it would be. Very slowly the girl paced forward.

"I have been talking with John. I'm sorry, but you cannot stay here."

Something died in Cary's heart. His surroundings blurred, began slowly to revolve. The face of Irma Sibley was a gray, ill-defined shape in a world of shadows. Words died on Cary's lips.

"Whatever you may or may not have done," the girl said coldly, "it is impossible for us to keep you here. God knows we have troubles enough of our own!"

CARY licked his dry lips, felt his tense face lose color. His shrug was a mechanical gesture. "I—understand." Abruptly he was breathing hard, both hands clamped on the edge of a table. "But I'm innocent! Good God, won't you believe that? They're accusing me of things I had nothing to do with!"

The answer came from outside, came in a ghostly wail from the slavering throats of ravenous hounds. That mad chorus, more than Cary's hoarse words, made the girl stiffen. Color seeped from her face; her eyes widened, filled with horror. Then suddenly her hands covered her face, and she was sobbing.

"Oh, God, I don't know what to do! If you go out there, you'll be killed! If you stay here and my father finds out—"

Another voice, Lannon Sibley's, found its way into the room, bellowing words of violence from somewhere nearby. Like the scraping of a tempered steel file on hard metal, the man's words rasped against Cary's eardrums.

In some nearby room, Lannon Sibley had flung open a window and was demanding of the assembled villagers what they meant by besieging his home. Guttural voices answered him from outside. Violent accusations were exchanged....

The window rasped shut. Heavy feet thumped across a threshold and pounded the corridor. Lannon Sibley's irate voice boomed out: "John! Irma! Where are you? Where *are* you, I say!"

The footsteps came closer to the room in which Cary Booth and the girl stood motionless. The girl's hand went to her mouth; her eyes filled with sudden terror. She flattened against the wall, stared at Cary and forced words from her lips. "Oh, God, if he finds you here—"

Cary jerked on the balls of his feet, frantically sought a hiding-

Inn of the Shadow-Creatures 81

place. But too late. Over the threshold came a tall, gaunt shape that stopped with a noisy suck of breath and stood glaring. Irma Sibley backed away from it, made a low sobbing sound. Gary returned the accusing glare of the man's ink-blot eyes and waited, fists clenched, body stiff as stone.

Something—something about Lannon Sibley was not real, not normal as human things should be normal. The thought crashed into Cary's brain with sledgehammer force. Staring into that face was like gazing through evil darkness into the bloodless features of a corpse come back to the world of living! The man's eyes were viscous bubbles of wet tar, glowing far back in ebony sockets. His flesh was watery white, strangely translucent.

Madness was in those eyes now. Madness tainted the words that snarled from Sibley's curled lips as he glared from Cary to Irma, took a stiff stride forward. "So—those beasts from the village were not lying!" His hands opened, closed convulsively like broken crabs. "What is the meaning of this? My daughter harboring a murderer?"

Irma Sibley sobbed an incoherent reply, fell away from him step by step and watched with terrified eyes as he advanced upon her. But the gaunt shape did not reach its objective. Cary Booth lunged sideways, planted himself wide-legged between the girl and her father. His lips curled, spilling thick words.

"Your daughter isn't protecting anyone! I came here of my own accord!" He sucked breath, let it growl through quivering nostrils. "And I'm leaving of my own accord, right now!"

"I—think—not!" One of those crawfish hands whipped down, clawlike fingers splayed open. Before Cary could leap forward, a blunt-nosed gun swung level with his chest, menaced him back again.

But the threat did not keep Irma Sibley from stumbling forward. Hands outflung, she pawed the gun aside, screamed into her father's twisted face: "No, no! You can't turn him over to those beasts! They'll kill him! You can't—"

The words gurgled in her throat as she staggered back, flung aside by Sibley's free hand. One of her high heels caught in the carpet, broke with a crackling sound and spilled her against the wall. Moaning, she slid to the floor, sat there like a small half-alive image of Buddha.

LANNON SIBLEY had put his filthy hands on the woman Cary loved! That thought, born of the hysteria in his heart, was mad in itself, but enough to smother any thought of self-preservation!

With blind fury Cary hurtled forward. Too late, Sibley jerked up the gun. Cary's flailing arm slammed it aside, tore it from the spiderleg fingers that gripped it. Next instant the two were pressed in mortal combat, straining, bunching the carpet beneath their straining feet.

Yet for Cary the conflict was weighted with savage odds. He fought terror as well as heaving flesh, fought madness along with the roaring, fuming bulk that sought to subdue him. The thing he battled was no human being! That leprous face belonged to no creature who rightfully walked the earth!

It was a death face, a mask of bloodless gelatin, too free from imperfections, too hairless, too void of blemishes to be real! It belonged on the robot-creation of some mad scientist, not on a human being possessed of God-given life!

Black fear chilled Cary's muscles, left him a prey to the slashing blows of Sibley's balled fists. Again and again those fists raked home, battered his sobbing lips, raised bulges beneath his gaping eyes. Blood blinded him, ran down the valley of his swollen tongue and seared the gas-burned membranes of his throat.

He fought frantically, with the dull realization that a black master of doom was squatting derisively on his laboring shoulders, leering at him, mocking his efforts. How—how in the name of God could any man battle a ghost-faced horror who had the strength of three men, who snarled and cursed and fought with the deliberate hacking fury of a trained killer?

How could any man fight a horrible thing out of hell, whose pale features were an inhuman mask of hate, whose hands were gaunt, bloodless claws possessed of diabolical strength?

Terror tore at Cary's heart, numbed him more than the staggering blows of his huge assailant. Paradoxically, terror produced madness and gave him strength to fight back! His own hands lashed up, ripped at the lean fingers that sought to seize his throat. His blunt nails raked flesh, flesh that was not flesh. He stared through a mist of horror... and one of Lannon Sibley's alabaster hands was no longer white but black! Black and deformed, like an acid-eaten claw....

The claw lunged at Cary's throat, clamped there—a shrunken black spider curling its hungry legs around a quivering victim. Horror mingled with festering terror in Cary's brain, congealed the blood in his veins. He fought mechanically to loosen the grip of the hideous hand, the hand that had been white as gypsum and now was black....

A knotted fist blurred through the blood-mist, bludgeoned against his face. Blood bubbled in his throat and he rocked backward, crashed against the table. The room revolved. Against the wall, Irma Sibley stared, screamed as if Cary Booth's agony were her own. From outside the house came a shrill ululation from restive man-hunters who sensed, perhaps, the nearness of their prey.

But Cary did not hear. Slowly, in agony, he sank into a bottomless pit of darkness, into a pool whose gurgling waters sucked him down to unconsciousness deep as death....

CHAPTER FOUR

The Monster's Choice

GUTTURAL VOICES aroused Cary Booth, dragged him back to a world peopled with muttering black demons. His body was a distorted thing racked with pain, having no form. Vaguely he was aware that Lannon Sibley stood in a doorway not far distant, saying harshly: "Take him! Take him and get out of here and leave me alone, you filthy beasts!"

Heavy hands dragged Cary to his feet and pushed him forward. No longer was he in the dimly lighted study of Lannon Sibley's strange house, hemmed in by four leering walls and menaced by creeping shadows. Cold air whipped his face; grass rustled under his stumbling feet. He was outside, had been carried out and flung to the muttering villagers.

More than that he could not tell. He could only lurch forward on stony legs, listening to the triumphant gutturals that rumbled like storm surf on all sides of him, staring into faces full of triumph.

The grass underfoot changed to the mud of a rutted road, the same road over which Cary Booth had hiked before. Cruel fingers kept their grip on his arms, forcing him forward. He walked like a dead man, feeling nothing.

When the wan lights of the village blinked ahead through a gray murk of dawn, he stared at them and shuddered, knowing that he had been dragged back, a prisoner, to the scene of the hideous crimes he had not committed.

Raindrops splashed his face as his captors dragged him across the square. Whining wind tugged at him, chilling him. Someone said throatily: "There's goin' to be a storm, Abel. That means the police'll be slow gettin' here."

As if in answer the gray sky opened; rain drenched Cary's body, thundered against his face and drove the shadows from his mind. He strained at the hands that held him, but the hands gripped harder, forced him up a flight of wooden steps. Above him the ancient sign with its sinister words *Red Hand Inn* creaked like a thing alive, leering evilly.

Then, prodded forward like a captured animal. Cary stumbled down the corridor into the sitting-room, staggered to a chair where cruel hands bound his arms and legs with ropes that this time would not allow him to escape.

He stared through half-closed eyes. The room was as dark, as shadow-ridden, as when he had left it—even darker now because of the storm brewing beyond its shuttered windows. Gas light made gaunt gargoyles of the accusing faces that glared at him. Slowly he peered from one face to another, saw the same grim leer.

Lannon Sibley had been right. The denizens of Troville were savage beasts who knew no compassion! Led by Abel Gravlin they had successfully tracked down their quarry and were waiting….

Gravlin scuffed forward like a monstrous toad. "This time you won't get away! God help you if you try it!"

The others nodded. Like members of some dark clan they moved their heads up and down, made muttering sounds that chilled Cary's heart. Words of protest sobbed to his lips, died there unuttered. What good would it do to swear his innocence? They would not believe him now even if he could produce proof!

He slumped wearily in his chair, ceased even to strain against the ropes that held him. The ropes this time had been knotted securely, wound so tightly that they burned the flesh of his wrists and ankles.

Somewhere a clock was ticking, and the sound was like the hollow thumping of a tortured heart. Cary turned his head, peered at the creeping clock-hands. Ten minutes after seven. How long before the police would come? There was no telling, now. Obviously, Lannon Sibley had allowed the villagers to use his phone, or else had phoned the police himself. They would come as quickly as possible. But this storm....

The gas flames flickered as wind shook the ancient house, moaning eerily through the walls. Rain beat a thunder-dirge overhead, jarring roof and walls, gnawing at shuttered windows. The police would be a long time. Meanwhile, the storm had brought a darkness deeper than night; the inn was a place of monstrous shadows, noisesome voices screaming through rooms and corridors....

THE clock ticked on. In the room with Cary, the villagers had resigned themselves to a long wait, had settled like weary hunters gloating over their captured prey. Cary shut his eyes, let his racked body go limp. This was the end—the end of everything. The police would come. Circumstantial evidence would brand him with the hideous murders committed by some unknown monster who even now might be lurking in the inn.

But whether or not they proved him guilty of those atrocities, it would not matter. Already they wanted him for another crime, for the murder of Bastone. That would be enough! Bastone's leering face would grin at him through the gloom of the death-house....

The hands of the clock moved on. Cary Booth groaned, stared again at his captors. Abel Gravlin was there, with his wife and moron son. Quentin Planchard, the real-estate man who hoped to buy property cheaply because of the new road. Mary Benson, whose sister had been butchered by the monster. Others... who lived in the village. And somewhere upstairs, lying ill in one of the storm-darkened rooms, would be Redfern, whom Mariah Gravlin believed to be a creature of darkness.

It would not be long. The police....

Cary's slumped body stiffened with a jerk. A dull *bong* had echoed through the room's silence as the clock struck the half hour. And from somewhere beyond the storm-racked room came an accompanying sound that whispered its way into the souls of the assembled villagers, freezing them with sudden expectation.

The voice rumbled into the room as if forced through thick lips by a squeezing of the spongy throat behind them. Increasing in volume it spewed forth a mad cacophony of unholy mirth. Louder and louder it howled its evil glee—and Cary Booth, rigid with terror, could almost see its owner's huge belly shaking.

Then, as if the handle of a siren were suddenly released and allowed to drag to a stop, the voice droned to silence. A scrape of slow footsteps sounded in the corridor beyond the room's closed door.

The occupants of the room were wooden images. None spoke, none moved. Abel Gravlin's ugly face, less than a yard from Cary's bulging eyes, turned ashen gray.

Slowly, step by step, the heavy feet in the corridor moved nearer, vibrating the floor with each dull thud. That sound, creeping into the tense bodies of those who heard it, was more soul-chilling than the wild cacophony that had preceded it. It boomed beneath the shrill whine of the storm. *Thud... thud... thud....*

The door creaked open as Cary Booth stared at it. A shriek welled against his clenched teeth, found utterance in a gurgling cry of horror. Within arm's reach of him Quentin Planchard lunged erect and staggered backward, sucking breath. Mary Benson screamed. Abel Gravlin sat rigid, gaping. Saul Gravlin, sitting crookedly on the floor with his head against his mother's fat legs, put an awkward hand to his witless face and scratched the side of his frowning mouth.

In the doorway, motionless against an ocher gas-glow from the corridor beyond stood a visitant from hell!

Cary's numbed brain reacted slowly. His eyes were glazed, squatting like round beetles in their dark sockets. Dully he associated the monster in the doorway with the madman whom he had battled in the musty den of Lannon Sibley's hellhouse. This intruder had the same gaunt frame and towering bulk.

But the creature could not be Sibley! The pin-point eyes that glowered through those oblong slits in the black head-covering were not Sibley's eyes. Ablaze with green hunger, they glared like the orbs of a slithering serpent!

The eyes crawled in their green pits, gazed about the room and missed nothing. Slowly the creature took a step forward, raised one black-clad arm until the splayed fingers of the extended hand were level with the terrified faces of his victims. His hidden lips sucked breath; his robed body swelled, seemed to lose earthly form. Cary Booth thought suddenly of the stricken man who was supposedly lying upstairs. Thought, with sickening terror, of Mariah Gravlin's harsh words: "He's one of them there vampires!"

Then, in a voice so low, so vibrant that it rustled the black mask, the monster was intoning ominous words:

"Be not afraid, ye who have gathered here to witness my coming. Be not afraid! I come only to deliver a warning and to claim a single victim from among you. There is nothing to fear... except for him whom I select to accompany me on my return to the pits of shadow!"

Soft laughter rumbled from the creature's masked lips. "Some of you who have lived long and are blessed with far-reaching memories may know who I am and from whence I come. It was written years ago, in the blood of a murdered woman, that the Red Hand Inn would fall into possession of those who dwell in darkness. It has been whispered that the shadow-creatures would return to claim their heritage....

"Ye have been warned! No longer may ye walk these rooms in peace! No longer may ye dwell here! That is the edict of the Brotherhood, and has been written in blood for ye to understand and obey! Again ye will be warned, and thereafter will no compassion be shown by me and mine. I come to claim a last victim! Take heed lest he be *not* the last!"

The black shape moved, paced with whispering steps toward the chair where Cary Booth sat rigid. Again the groping hand reached out, and a snaky forefinger pointed ominously into Cary's face.

"Ye may go, all of you! Go, and leave this hapless creature in my care. Go—*and do not return!*"

CARY BOOTH surged frantically at the bonds that held him. Wide-eyed, he gazed into the monster's advancing mask, and suddenly a mighty hope surged through him.

What manner of face lay behind that concealing mask? Was it in truth a face born of hell, the hideous countenance of some uncouth demon risen from inferno?

Or was it the face of a *friend?* Back there in Lannon Sibley's home the girl and her brother had sought to protect him from the people of the village! They had failed through no fault of their own. Was this a desperate attempt to turn that failure into success?

Stiff as stone, Cary watched the demon's slow movements, listened to the throaty words from behind the mask.

"Go... and do not return! This is the abode of the dwellers of darkness, forbidden to ye who have not yet crossed the Black Master's threshold! Go...."

Into Cary's throat came a peal of wild laughter that he stifled with a mighty effort. He was right! There could be no other answer. This thing was a mad mummery created for his benefit!

And the mummery was working! Even now the assembled villagers clawed at one another in their eagerness to escape.

Vaguely, Cary realized that Abel Gravlin and his followers were gone, gone in blind terror, like frightened children fleeing the presence of a thing they could not understand. But *he* understood! And when they learned the truth they would curse themselves for being fools!

The ticking of the clock, again audible, was smothered by the half-hysterical laughter that jangled from Cary's lips. He stared into the featureless face of the creature who stood over him.

"It worked!" he shrieked. "It worked! For God's sake, cut me loose and let's get out of here—whoever you are!"

"Yes." The monster's reply came in a low chuckle. "They may come back. When they do, it will be too late."

Black hands fumbled with the ropes that bound Cary's arms to the chair. They were patient, those hands, and slow moving. A sob of relief choked in Cary's throat as the ropes loosened. The sob changed to a sucking intake of breath as something else, something cold and sharp, closed with a dull click over his aching wrists. He tried to wrench his hands free.

The robed monster stepped back, chuckling with vile mirth.

The green-glowing eyes gloatingly watched every changing expression of Cary's face.

And Cary's face did change. Hope went out of it as his blood turned to water. Terror returned to his numbed heart and was a hundred times more unbearable because of the wild hope that had preceded it. His body sagged. He stared dully at his tormentor and had no strength left even to make words. The steel bands that encircled his wrists were shackles... and the fiend's black hands were cruelly clamping a second pair of bracelets around his bound ankles!

"Yes, they may come back," the monster chuckled. "But when they do it will be too late. Too—late! You thought I was a creature of this earth, come to save you. Soon you will know better!"

Strong arms lifted Cary from the chair, enfolded his trembling body as the tentacles of an octopus might have coiled about the body of something to be crushed and devoured. Still chuckling, the monster turned, carried his victim across the shadowed room and climbed the gaslit staircase leading to the floor above. Just once Cary struggled in that cruel embrace, but the struggle was half-hearted. No man whose legs were clamped together, whose hands were shackled behind his back, could hope to squirm from the grip of those black-clad arms!

At the head of the stairs the monster turned, paced slowly along the upper hall toward the chamber where Cary had long ago carried a naked, stupefied shape named Redfern. The door was closed now. A thrust of the fiend's foot jarred it open. Silently the monster carried his burden over the threshold, kicked the door shut and flung Cary Booth to the floor.

The impact jarred Cary loose from the pall of terror that had numbed him. Agony went through his shoulders as he writhed over on his back, stared dully at his surroundings. The eyes behind the mask leered down at him. And Cary knew, knew with sudden soul-retching dread, the identity of that hidden face!

Hours ago he had left Redfern sprawled in an insensate heap on the bed in this very chamber. That bed would be empty now. Mariah Gravlin had been right....

He turned his head, dragged himself to his knees and stared.

And the bed was not empty. On it lay a limp, silent figure whose head was turned so that Cary could gaze into chalk-like features.

He stared for ten seconds. Then with a shudder that racked his whole frame he tried to lunge erect, stumble forward. For the thing on the bed was not Redfern. It was the limp, near-naked, unconscious form of Irma Sibley!

CHAPTER FIVE

THE SHADOW CREATURE

*S*PURRED ON by sudden madness, Cary hurled himself at the bed, forgot the steel shackles that encircled his ankles. The shackles spilled him, flung him headlong. Sobbing, he crashed against the bedpost, sprawled on the crumpled covers with his face but inches from the girl's. A sickly sweet stench of chloroform hung about Irma Sibley's nose and lips. Desperately, Cary wriggled away.

Black hands clawed his trembling body and flung him aside. Once again the floor crashed into him. He lay limp, staring, waiting for the inevitable. Escape this time was impossible. He was utterly helpless to fight, either for himself or for the girl he loved....

The door was closed, the room illuminated by a single sputtering gas-jet that protruded from the wall above the bed. Here in the upper part of the house the voice of the storm was a wailing shriek. But the terror-scream in Cary Booth's heart was an unuttered sound of madness. Welling into his throat it gurgled there, became a hoarse sob as the robed monster turned to look at him.

The demon's eyes were tiny pin-heads of malice, green-glowing with triumph.

"You see, my friend, we will not be interrupted. Hours will pass before Abel Gravlin—" He mouthed the name as if it tasted good—"and the others will dare return. Then, do you know what they will find?"

Cary had no reply. His racked body pressed hard against the wall beneath a window that rattled to the impact of driving rain.

Frantically he strove to wrench his hands from the bracelets.

"They will find *this!*" Slowly the monster turned, leaned above the bed and put black hands on Irma Sibley's inert body. His cruel fingers fastened in the girl's garments, burst the cloth and ripped it from top to bottom, exposing satin-smooth flesh. Gloating over the object of his attack, he turned the girl's limp body as a dressmaker might turn a wire-framed dummy in order to remove silken undergarments, bits of pink lace....

Naked, she lay beneath the hungry glare of those green-glowing eyes; but the girl was unaware of her nakedness, mercifully oblivious to the defiling touch of the fiend's hands.

"She is lovely, no?" Like a huge robot the gowned monster turned again to peer at Cary. "She is young and sweet. When she has joined those of us who dwell beyond the gates of shadow, she will be a beautiful member of our dark company. As for you—" He paced forward, stood above Cary's shackled body and peered down, his eyes full of cold mirth. "You are in love with her! Why deny it? It is written in your face, in your eyes!"

"Damn you, yes!" With sudden fury, Cary heaved himself to his knees, found courage to return the man's unholy glare. "I'm in love with her! If you lay—"

"You are in love with her. That makes it all the more beautiful. When Gravlin and the others return they will say with ecstacy, 'Ah, see the charming lovers! See how they embrace each other even in death! Is it not beautiful, their last loving embrace?'"

Evil laughter gurgled in the fiend's throat. "And then—" His voice grew cold, ominous— "they will forget the beauty of it. They will realize that you and she are—dead!" His triumphant mirth became an obscene chuckle. "But you expected to die even when you came here, did you not? Even when you came to the inn and said your name was Henry Smith? You had murdered a man. The fear of death was in your heart, in your eyes! You expected to be dragged back."

Cary's reply was a gurgling explosion of breath, incoherent. Black hands reached beneath the folds of the fiend's flowing robe, came out again gripping a ragged strip of paper.

"This is irony, my friend. Fate laughs at you. In fear of your life you fled from the pursuing phantom of death and came here. Now you are about to die... but if you had not fled in terror from the scene of your crime, you would not be here, and you would not now be on the grim threshold of death! Look at this." The black hands stabbed downward, thrusting the paper before Cary's eyes. "Look how bitterly ironic fate can be!"

Cary stared. The ragged strip of paper was from a newspaper. Black letters leered back into his wide-eyed gaze.

Mechanically he read:

Alfred Bastone... completely recovered from his mystery-attack by an unknown assailant... has announced his intention of departing for Europe on an extended vacation. Your Keyhole Columnist believes, deep down under, that Mr. Bastone fears a second visit from the unknown and, for reasons of his own, desires to be many miles from New York when the nameless one calls again....

Cary Booth's head jerked up; his gaunt face filled with surging relief. "Then I didn't kill him! Oh, thank God! They're not after me any more! I'm free! *Free!*"

His shrill voice reverberated like crackling thunder through the rooms. Wildly he surged up from the floor.

Black hands thrust him down again. Green-glowing eyes glared at him mockingly. "That is the irony of fate, my friend. *They* do not want you, but my people do. You fled from an imaginary hell into a real one. And now—"

THE fiend's claws stabbed down and reached under Cary's armpits, hauling him erect. Once again he was hurled forward, this time with such force that the shackles ate like hot flame into his ankles. Stumbling headlong, he sprawled on the bed, felt his face sink with bruising force into the warm satin of Irma Sibley's body. And the hands followed him, closed over his tortured arms and flung him sprawling on the crumpled bed-covers beside the girl who lay there.

The green-glowing eyes were close to Cary's face. He stared up into them, shuddered with a sudden mental vision that stormed his brain. This room was not a musty chamber in the Red Hand Inn; it was a torture-vault in some subterranean hell!

A numbness as to death itself claimed Cary's heart. The very touch of the monster's hands was unreal. Dully, Cary was aware that the clawlike fingers were tearing at his clothing, stripping him…. Cruelly they raked his flesh, tugged at him viciously till he was as naked as the girl who lay motionless beside him.

"You love her," the monster chuckled. "Yes, that is beautiful. Side by side, you and she will lie, your bodies united in sleep. Your blood will mingle with hers, to pay for the blood of those who died in this accursed place years ago…."

He stepped backward, turned silently and paced beneath the sputtering ocher glow of the gas-jet. A shadowed corner of the room sucked him into its dark embrace, curled like a black winding-sheet about him while he gathered up a pair of sinister objects that leaned against the wall. When he returned to the bed, two significant tools lay in his hands—one of them an iron-headed sledge, the other a sharpened steel stake, long and thick as a tall man's cane.

"Yes, you and she shall lie together in your happiness. Your body against hers, your arms embracing her. And this—" His black fingers caressed the stake—"to impale you both, binding you together in an embrace of death. Then when Gravlin and his tribe return, they will look upon you and say, 'What a lovely couple! How beautiful their affection for each other!'

"But first, my friend, I must relieve your suffering. When you enter our world of whispering darkness you must come in peace, lest you disturb the shadows that wait to embrace you…."

Cary Booth stared in horror, stared with white-rimmed eyes as the monster's hands disappeared with dread significance into the folds of the black robe. Reappearing, those hands held a small glass vial and a sponge. Carefully soaking the sponge with the vial's liquid contents, the demon leaned forward, leered down again.

"It will take but a moment, that is all. Then you will sleep deeply in the arms of your loved one. And when the stake pierces the small of your back, to pass through you and invade the smooth loveliness of her body… you will perhaps not even feel the pain of it!"

The black hand reached down, stabbed toward Cary's bloodless lips. The sickly reek of chloroform choked his nostrils, seeped into his throat.

And then, with madness born of frantic fear, Cary moved.

His hands were shackled beneath him, pressed hard against his back. With a superhuman effort he heaved his thigh upward, hooked his knees. His shackled feet shot out and up like twin pistons!

Mad strength lay behind that thrust. Animal cunning blazed in Cary's bulging eyes. The solid flesh of his bare heels made grinding contact with the fiend's black face—slammed the face backward with such savage force that the man's neck seemed to be made of rubber.

The sponge dropped from paralyzed fingers. As if struck by a battering ram the monster reeled backward, went off balance and crashed to the floor, skidding as his twisted body made contact with a ragged square of carpet.

Before he could heave himself erect, Cary was on him. Head foremost, he had hurtled through space. Agony streaked through him as he crashed into the black-haired body. But his knees found the man's face, smashed home. His bare shoulders writhed on the floor and his shackled feet, like the heads of two striking snakes, battered the face and chest, wrung shrieks from masked lips.

DULLY, through a blood-haze that blurred his brain, Cary realized that someone in the room was shrilling a wild cacophony of gibbering laughter. Then he knew that the laughter was spilling from his own lips, welling from his own heart!

"So you're human! You're human after all and you can be killed the same as any other human! Take *that,* damn you! And *that!* And *that!*"

He stopped screaming. He had realized that his stabbing feet were no longer grinding against the monster's writhing body. And when his triumphant shrieks ceased, another sound was audible. Slow footsteps—in the corridor outside....

Cary squirmed on the floor, wrenched his head up and stared. The robed fiend had groped erect—stood swaying on widespread legs!

He was staring at Cary but listening to the alien sounds from the corridor. One of his robed arms was half extended toward the iron sledge on the bed. He seemed undecided whether to seize the sledge and beat Cary's half-erect body to Unconsciousness... or to turn and flee.

The footsteps in the corridor came near.

Cary moved before the monster reached a decision. Lunging erect on shackled legs, he hurtled forward. His lowered head ground into the man's abdomen, sank into heaving flesh. The black hands stabbed down with frantic quickness.

The hands raked Cary's naked shoulders, sought his throat. They missed their mark. Cary's teeth raked one of the black wrists, sank through the opaque covering and dug into quivering flesh. Gasping a scream of sudden agony, the man wrenched his hands free....

The black covering ripped loose, hung dangling from Cary's closed mouth. And the hand beneath that covering, the exposed hand that flailed empty space as the demon lunged backward, was not black but white—white and human!

With a sobbing suck of breath the monster leaped, hurled himself at the closed door. His clawing fingers wrenched it open. He swirled across the threshold and lunged into the gaslit corridor.

Swaying on spread knees, Cary Booth glared in triumph at the empty doorway. Blood flecked his lips, stained the rubbery stuff that dangled from his clenched teeth. A stink of chloroform hung in his throat.

The wound in his side was open again and throbbing viciously. The room refused to be still; floor and walls and ceiling made an endless revolving wheel, and in the center of the scarlet maze stood a blurred shape that was a bed... an ill-defined shadow-ridden bed where lay the alabaster form of a woman.

That woman was alive. Alive! The black-robed visitant from hell had failed!

A glad cry choked in Cary's soul. He heaved himself erect, moved with short jerky steps to the door. The humped threshold threatened to spill him as he twisted his shackled feet over it. Then in the corridor outside, he stood stock still, gaping.

Only a single gas-jet was burning, and that glowed near the head of the stairs like a baleful yellow eye.

There in the ocher pool of light stood a thin, stoop-shouldered shape, staring at him. The face above that matchstick body, peering in halfwit bewilderment at Cary Booth's manacled legs, was that of Saul Gravlin, the moron son of the retired chemistry-professor who owned this dark house of hell!

A crooked smile curled Cary's lips. The shuffling footsteps of a sixteen-year-old halfwit had saved two lives! Unknowingly, Saul Gravlin had frightened away a demon who with one blow could have hurled the boy into annihilation!

Mad mirth gurgled on Cary's lips and died there with a sudden contracting of his throat muscles. His gaze leaped past the half wit, focused on something else—on a black, bloated shape that loomed in shadows at the deep end of the corridor!

CARY screamed. The moron son of Abel and Mariah Gravlin turned with a convulsive jerk and stood rigid, gripping the banister at the staircase head. Not more than twenty paces distant, in midnight gloom at the corridor's end, a black ghoul-shape moved slowly forward, its hideous face leering above an ill-defined, shapeless torso. The same horrific monstrosity that Cary Booth had seen once before....

Cary's wide eyes saw only the face, and the face was a grinning death's-head swaying toward him. Flinging both hands out to ward off the almost tangible wave of evil that swirled against him, Cary stumbled backward.

But the horror had no numbing effect on the halfwit who stood at the stairhead. Scowling darkly, Saul Gravlin returned the glare of the corpse-face without so much as a shudder. Slowly he scuffed forward, stopped again and stood wide-legged. One of his dangling arms jerked up. The outstretched hand gripped a revolver!

"Listen, you!" Saul rasped. "You ain't murderin' no one else. You're done!"

The gun leaped like a living thing in his fingers, hurled out a thunder-roar that choked the passage. The corpse-face stiffened in sudden agony, vile lips writhed open, spewed forth a gurgling choking sound that mingled with the dying echoes of the revolver. Then the black hulk swayed forward, arched downward through gloom and thudded to the floor. Retching, it writhed up again a few inches and sank in an agony of death.

Said Gravlin grinned from ear to ear, made chuckling sounds as he scuffed forward. Like a robot, Cary trailed after him, pawing the corridor wall. It was Cary who sank beside the gargoyle face and gaped into it.

The face was human. It was hideous, blotchy with grafted skin and scarred flesh, and made even more hideous by the gaping bullet hole that seemed to have squashed its hooked nose to one side—but it was human, not a mask. And the monster's large body, garbed in dark clothing which had blurred against the blackness was human, too....

Cary muttered aloud: "He—he took off the robe and mask and—and—" He rocked backward, jerked his head around and rasped at Saul Gravlin: "Listen. He's got the keys to these shackles. I can't use my hands to find them. Help me!"

The halfwit was still grinning. A slight shudder went through him as he leaned forward, but the grin clung to his lips. He pawed through the dead man's clothing, scowled, straightened with a shrug. "There ain't no keys."

"There must be! Look again!"

The halfwit looked again. "Nope, there ain't none."

Cary groaned, knew the answer. The manacles had come from a pocket in the monster's robe. The keys would be in the same pocket. They had to be! But after fleeing, the fiend had rid himself of robe and mask....

Cary bent closer, went off balance and would have fallen across the man's bloody gargoyle-face if Saul had not caught him. Something about that face was familiar, horribly familiar even in the winding-sheet of darkness that enveloped it. Cary's gaze focused on the man's gloved hands.

Then abruptly he remembered the naked, chloroformed shape that lay in the torture-room. Cold terror stormed his brain, terror caused by a wave of black intuition that swept over him. He shuddered erect, lurched on stiff legs and lunged forward, forgetting the shackles on his ankles.

The steel bands ate into raw flesh, spilled him as effectively as if the dead man had reached out and gripped his legs. Other bracelets held his arms behind him, kept him from jerking them forward to break his fall. Headlong he sprawled forward, down.

Saul Gravlin reached out to clutch him and missed. The floor of the corridor came up like a flat black bludgeon and crashed against Cary's face. He moaned, rolled over in dull agony. The dark ceiling above him heaved as if alive. The single sputtering gas-jet, burning near the stairhead a dozen yards distant, became a baleful red-ringed monster-eye—and slowly blinked out....

CHAPTER SIX

The Monster Returns

THE RASPING sound of steel scraping against steel jarred Cary out of unconsciousness, lifted him into a shadowed world of torment. Heavy hammers beat a dirge macaber inside his throbbing head; a mist swam before his eyes. Ankles and wrists were on fire and clutching fingers were inside him, seeking his soul.

Lights blurred through the black pall and droning voices welled into being. Cary groaned, turned his racked body. The rasping sound ceased and a throaty voice intoned: "He's comin' to. Thank God for that much, anyhow! Now, if Sibley's son will only get here—"

Cary stared into a round red moon of face, at the blue serge of a police uniform. He sighed, turned his head farther around and gaped at his surroundings. The thing that held him was a musty divan, and the room was the same sitting-room where, twice before, he had been held prisoner.

Was he a prisoner now?

"Hold still, mister," the policeman ordered. "About a minute more and we'll have these bracelets off."

The rasping sound began again, made by a steel file grinding against the stubborn metal of the shackles on Cary's wrists. He moaned with relief when the cuffs came loose. Clawing the policeman's shoulder he sat up, leaned against the arm of the divan. The manacles at his ankles had already been removed.

Faces stared at him. Abel Gravlin's face, Mariah's, Quentin Planchard's... all the faces which not long ago had been loaded with hate. But there was no hate in them now.

Suddenly Cary gripped the policeman's arm, dug hard fingers into it. "Where's Irma? Is she—"

The man pointed. Across the room in a shadowed corner where the flickering glow of gas-jets barely penetrated, a sobbing figure was hunched above something that lay stiff and motionless on a couch. Cary stood up, stumbled forward. The girl stared at him as he approached.

She turned her tear-stained face away and Cary gaped down at the thing beside her. He shuddered. It was the thing he had encountered in the corridor upstairs, eternities ago. Up there, darkness had blurred the shattered face. Gas light was in it now, revealing every fearful feature.

Blood congealed in Cary's veins and he stood rigid, eyes bulging. The face had been familiar before, in veiling shadows. Now—now it was doubly familiar. That unsightly countenance, beet-red with patches of grafted skin, gaunt with deep pits of shrunken flesh.

Cary's eyes closed to blot out the horror. Slowly the truth ate into him and he knew why Irma Sibley was sobbing over a dead thing that possessed a face of macaber ugliness.

His thoughts went sluggishly back to the home of Lannon Sibley, to the black memory of his own combat with the girl's father. Something had been strange, horribly unreal…something about Lannon Sibley's too-white, too-smooth face and hands. Now—he knew.

This thing lying rigid in death was the man he had fought! This unlovely gargoyle was Lannon Sibley's true face, and those gnarled blackened claws were his true hands. The other had been a mask, to hide what lay beneath. A mask of some rubbery, fleshy substance, to cover the horror!

Cary's flesh crawled; hair bristled on his neck. He turned slowly, walked back to where Abel Gravlin and the others where silently watching him. He said dully: "What—happened?"

"The police came," Gravlin shrugged, "and had courage enough to enter this accursed place. They found my son upstairs in the hall, trying to shake you back to consciousness. And they found

Lannon Sibley. My son says he shot him!"

"He did." Cary Booth sank wearily into a chair. "Yes, he—did."

"We are waiting now for John Sibley. He has been notified."

Cary sat motionless, aware that the room was still alive with the drone of savage rain. The storm had not abated; windows still rattled and the inn was an abode of evil whispers and dismal creaking sounds that made his flesh creep. The clock on the sitting-room wall ticked sluggishly.

Another sound invaded the room. Outside, a car had stopped; the door of the inn groaned open and footsteps echoed hollowly in the hall. Cary pulled his head up and stared at John Sibley as Sibley came over the threshold.

The man was drenched, disheveled, his face a gaunt mask racked with torment. As if walking in sleep he paced forward, stared around the room. Words choked in his throat. "Where is he? Oh God—!"

He saw his sister and walked toward her, stood like a figure in some shadowy wax-museum while he gazed down into his father's face. A shudder began in his legs and ran to his sagging shoulders. When he turned away, his face was bloodless, his hands and lips twitching.

The uniformed policeman who had entered the room with him strode forward, tossed a paper-wrapped package on the table and swung to the moon-faced officer in charge. "I been talking to him." He jerked a thumb at John. "That's why we were so long gettin' here."

He would have said more, but the son of Lannon Sibley sank into a chair, stared with watery eyes and mumbled thickly: "I—feel responsible for all the terrible things that have happened! Oh my God, if I had only realized!"

ABEL GRAVLIN and the others leaned forward, hanging on Sibley's words. But Cary Booth ignored those words, centered his attention, instead, on every changing expression of the innkeeper's face and every furtive movement made by Quentin Planchard. John Sibley's mumbled explanations would not bring the affairs of the Red Hand Inn to a close! The others thought so. But Gary Booth knew better....

Sibley, on the verge of hysterics, clawed the chair-arms with sweat-drenched hands and made an effort to shake loose the horror that gripped him. "I should have known! God forgive me, I should have been less blind from the very beginning!" He shuddered, shut his eyes as if to blot out a hideous memory. "But my father had acted so strangely for so long, ever since the terrible accident that burned his face and hands. He was never the same after that. He wanted to be left alone, and grew to hate the sight of normal human beings—even Irma and me. Even the mask he wore, the mask that was made for him by a specialist, did not change him. At times he was not—not sane."

Sibley's voice husked on, sobbing its way through the moan of storm-wind and the slow ticking of the clock. "It was because of my father that we came to Troville to live. He wanted to be away from people. And when we did come here he grew worse, refusing even to leave the house. He learned to hate Irma and me—he was going mad...."

"But I should have known! Oh God, if I had only realized what he meant, the day he talked with me about buying the inn. He—he came into my den while I was working, and he sat there and talked, talked on and on about what he meant to do. His idea was to give the inn a reputation and then buy it. You know, there will be a new state road through here in a few months. My father thought the inn would be a tremendous money-making proposition if he could build up its weird reputation. He talked about it that afternoon, he wanted to make a ghost-house of the place, combining ancient legends and gruesome tales with new—new horrors!"

"You'll swear to that?" the moon-faced officer demanded.

"I don't need to." Sibley buried his face in his hands, raised it again convulsively. "The afternoon he came into my den, I was working. The dictaphone was running and—and when I saw the unholy eagerness on his face, I forgot to shut the machine off. Our conversation is recorded on the disc there." He aimed a trembling forefinger at the paper-wrapped package on the table.

"That's what took us so long." The officer who had accompanied Sibley to the inn leaned forward, nodding. "I told him what'd happened and—well, after the shock kind of died down, he rummaged around in his den to find the record. He played it for me. It's what he says it is, all right."

"Oh God, if I had only realized at the time! If I had only known how terribly far his madness had progressed...."

Moon-face nodded, peered across the room to where Irma Sibley sat in silence beside the horror-faced corpse of her father. "I guess you and your sister better go home, Mr. Sibley. We can get the rest of it later." He stood up, dragged a noisy breath. "We'll just drape a sheet over the body there until the medical examiner gets a look at it."

Dispassionately he turned to Cary Booth. "You, young feller, you're in pretty bad shape. If you want medical attention you can come along with us."

Cary Booth's answer came slowly. Staring into the halfwit face of Saul Gravlin, a face that still bore a significant, suggestive grin, he said almost inaudibly: "I'll—stay—here."

And though the others looked at him in astonishment he sat where he was, unmoving. The uniformed policemen went out. John and Irma Sibley walked together to the door.

At the threshold, the girl turned her head, stared at Cary with damp dark eyes that seemed to hold a message.

Others left the room and still Cary sat motionless. The ordeal over? He knew better. He had seen things the others had not seen—knew things they did not know.

No, the hideous procession of horrors was not yet finished. Somewhere in this evil abode of shadows lurked a strange naked shape named Redfern, who had been left ill in one of the upstairs rooms and had then disappeared! Somewhere, too, lay a black robe and black head-covering, discarded by a murdering monster *who had not yet been caught!*

The ordeal was over. John Sibley and the others were wrong in thinking so! Terribly wrong! Other persons could have had the same motive as Lannon Sibley for desiring to turn the Red Hand Inn into a horror-house. Quentin Planchard, for instance. And Abel Gravlin, who may or may not have come here to escape the shame of an unfortunate marriage. And other persons could have had other motives....

Alone, Cary Booth stared around him, felt worms of dread creep again into his heart as the room's crawling shadows closed around him. For the present he was free to come and go as he pleased. But he could not leave. Before long the nameless monster of Red Hand Inn would return to perpetrate new crimes; and then because of circumstantial evidence, Cary Booth would again be blamed. The monster would return, would strike and vanish—and Cary Booth would be dragged back, if *still alive*, and branded anew!

The villagers were wrong. In their ignorance they had left the way open, unguarded, for the demon of Troville to return!

THE clock ticked on.... Footsteps, murmuring voices, had long ago died to silence and the inn's occupants had sought the seclusion of their own rooms. Gusts of wind-driven rain beat a nerve-racking dirge against loose window panes.

Cary stood up, paced silently across the room and climbed the stairs. No sound greeted him as he prowled into the upper corridor. The inn seemed as deserted now as it had a little while ago. The same ocher flame-tongue flickered at the stairhead.

The room where Cary Booth and Irma Sibley had so nearly shared a last embrace was empty. A thorough search disclosed nothing of importance. Frowning, Cary stepped again into the corridor and began a systematic, patient search of every chamber not occupied by Abel Gravlin's guests.

Probably the police, too, had searched these rooms....

A match sputtered in Cary's outthrust hand and he crossed a threshold, closed a door behind him and touched the flame to a gas-jet. A closed closet door faced him. He paced forward.

His hand touched the knob and he stepped back, looked down. Breath whined in his throat. At his feet something red and wet snaked beneath the door.

His fingers went cold on the knob, slowly turned it. Then his eyes widened, protruded from their dark sockets. The thing before him was a clothes-closet, deep enough for crawling shadows to blur the inner wall. Against that wall hung a shape that was human!

A second match sputtered and the glare leaped forward to disclose the niche's contents. The thing that hung there, arms rigid and feet dangling inches above the floor, was stark naked. The same stark naked form that Cary Booth had long ago seen prowling through the hall!

Redfern! But Redfern would never again creep like a hungry ghost through darkness. The man's eyes were glass marbles, his tongue a bloated thing too large for his mouth. Ropes bound his wrists to a high cross-beam. Some heavy instrument, perhaps a steel stake, had pierced his naked body and blood had dripped… dripped…. Redfern! And the man had been dead a long while. Hours!

Cary stepped back, dragged his gaze from the corpse and turned to pace across the room. In the corridor he jarred to a stop. An open door loomed just ahead. Through it came a sound that tensed the muscles in his throat, choked his breath. In the chamber beyond that open doorway a window had creaked!

The window ceased to creak and something heavy thudded to the floor. Cary jerked backward, flattened in shadows. Footsteps whispered across the room; a dark shape, darker than the gloom of the corridor, prowled stealthily over the threshold, seemed to hesitate a moment and then turned furtively, went cat-footing along the hall.

Cary watched with unblinking eyes, felt the cords of his neck stand out. The prowling shape was moving away from him, its back toward him. Again it hesitated, seemed to listen warily for sounds, of impending danger. Silently it slid across the corridor, inched a door open and vanished.

A creaking sound, as of unoiled castors worming across an uncarpeted floor, squeaked through the silence. The sound ceased; returning footsteps jarred the floor. In the doorway the prowling shape reappeared.

It was not the same shape. Staring at it, Cary Booth felt his eyes widen With abrupt terror, felt a sudden cold chill stab through his rigid body. The thing that stood now in the doorway, looming there like a bloated visitant from some dark hell, was all too familiar!

The monster had returned!

BREATH whined through Cary's lips and the sound stiffened that bloated black shape in its tracks. Like a huge bat the monster whirled.

It was too late then for Cary Booth to leap sideways, conceal himself in shadows, even had he desired to. But no such desire festered in his brain. An animal snarl spewed from his throat and he hurtled forward, drove his bent body straight at the hell-spawned thing in front of him.

This time his wrists and ankles were free of torturing steel bands. The odds no longer stood top-heavy against him!

He struck with the force of a flung boulder, slammed his head and shoulders into the black hulk's belly and raked upward with clenched fists. Breath exploded from the fiend's throat.

Human or not, the monster staggered back under that savage onslaught! His feet scraped the floor; the wall of the passage ground into him, stopped him with a jolt. Arms outflung, he fought desperately to keep Cary's flailing fists at bay.

Cary spilled down, locked both arms around the robed legs and heaved!

It was enough. With a lurid scream the robed one lunged off balance, writhed in space and rumped the floor with such force that the windows rattled in a nearby room. Cary plunged headlong, crushed the squirming shape beneath him. Obsessed with animal fury he gripped the black throat in both hands, wrenched it up and slammed it down again with a ramrod-stiffening of his corded arms.

The masked head made crunching contact. A sob bubbled behind black cloth. The monster sucked breath, emptied his lungs in a whispering groan and lay still.

Triumph made scarlet flame-pits of Cary's eyes. He reached down, fastened curled fingers in the black head-covering. Beneath his straddled legs, the bloated shape lay motionless.

Then he knew his mistake. Black hands raked up, smashed

against his face! The corpse found life, heaved sideways with a rolling sweep that hurled Cary Booth against the wall.

The black fingers clung to their objective, dug like steel hooks into the tortured flesh of Cary's neck. With strength born of blood-hungry madness the monster slammed his victim to the floor, writhed atop him and squeezed vicious thumbs against Cary's jugular.

Breath rattled in Cary's throat, burned his lips as it wheezed through them. His eyes bulged; blood boiled in his face. Death stared down at him with smouldering eyes that glared through oblong slits in the mask. Bony knees ground into his abdomen, torturing him.

One of the black hands released its throttling grip and snaked upward, stabbed into the dark folds of the fiend's garment. Slithering clear, the hooked fingers held a gun. Cary Booth's bulging eyes filled with soul-freezing fear as the gun-muzzle gazed hollowly down into his face.

Cold sweat broke out on his forehead. He stopped writhing, lay stiff as stone. This—was the end. Numbness crawled into him and he no longer felt the agony inflicted by the fiend's crushing knees, no longer knew the pressure of black fingers that stabbed his throat. The end, after all, was to be death. In a moment the monster's trigger-finger would tighten....

It tightened.

With a last despairing effort that racked his tortured body from head to foot, Cary Booth jerked his head aside. But there was no explosion from the menacing revolver above him. The fiend's forefinger had pressed the trigger, but there was no explosion!

Instead, a hissing stream of smoke colored gas spewed from the gun-muzzle. Gas! The same gray horror that had snaked under the door of Cary Booth's room, eternities ago, seeking to annihilate him!

The stream missed its mark, flattened against the floor instead of searing Cary's bloodless face. His writhing body doubled at the belt; his legs whipped up, clamped with vicious strength around the neck of the monster above him. They raked down again, dragged the demon with them. Black fingers lost their torture-grip on Cary's throat as the robed shape tumbled over backward.

Next instant Cary's stabbing hand had wrenched the gun out and down, ripped it from the claws that held it. His clenched fist clubbed the fiend's hidden face, slammed the man against the corridor wall. Hooked fingers ripped the mask, bared the white flesh beneath.

A shriek of stark terror shrilled from the man's throat as the gun shot down. But Cary Booth had no compassion, no mercy. Already his eyes were on fire, his throat choked with deadly fumes. In another moment the fumes would take effect in full force....

Again his knotted fist smashed into the fiend's screaming face. Then the gun-muzzle lashed down, broke teeth as it buried itself in the man's writhing mouth. Cary's finger squeezed the trigger....

When he swayed backward, the face beneath him was a gargoyle blue with death. The eyes were swollen black balls too big for their sockets. The gaping mouth was a well of crawling gray gas-fumes.

But the face, despite its hideous distortion, was recognizable....

Footsteps pounded the staircase and Cary jerked his head, stared. A sobbing voice spilled his name. White hands clawed the banister; Irma Sibley came stumbling along the hall. Cary gaped, then abruptly reached down and drew the torn black mask over the dead man's face.

It would not do for Irma Sibley to—to look into that face. The face was hideous in death... and the black-robed monster was Irma Sibley's brother!

Slowly, Cary swayed erect, stepped forward. His arms were out when the girl reached him. Sobbing, sobbing with the joy of finding him alive, she flung herself into his embrace.

LATER in the downstairs room of the inn, Irma Sibley sat in a musty chair and looked into faces that were gaunt in the ocher glare of flickering gas-jets. She stared at a moon-faced man in uniform and shuddered. She ceased to shudder when Cary Booth, beside her, put his arm about her shoulders and said quietly: "You mustn't be afraid. Tell them the truth."

The girl said slowly: "John was not—my brother. He was father's stepson. He has always hated dad, hated him terribly. He was a terribly spoiled youth and father refused to give him money unless he earned it. All father's money was to be his and mine when father died, but until then he had to work for what little he got. He hated father for that. Hated him and watched him and was always waiting—waiting for the time when he might have revenge."

She closed her eyes and her hot slender fingers gripped Cary's arm, seeking strength. Talking to those staring faces was an ordeal. "John must have laid his plans when father first began talking about buying the inn. He saw a way then to get rid of dad and come into the money. He began by spreading hints around that father was strange, even—mad. Then he made that dictaphone recording. I—I don't know what is on the disc, but I'm sure it's innocent. Father did plan to give the inn a creepy reputation, and the recording may sound as if he were deliberately planning to commit real crimes, but he wasn't! I *know* he wasn't! My father wasn't wicked. He was just a poor bewildered man whom fate treated terribly!"

"Then you think, Miss Sibley," the moon-faced policeman said quietly, "that John committed these crimes knowing that your father would be blamed for them."

"Yes," the girl whispered.

"But your father came here to the inn often. He was slain here."

"He came because he knew John was up to something!" Irma Sibley clenched her hands and leaned forward. "Why shouldn't he come? He wanted to know what his hateful stepson was doing! And when he came here, he removed his—his artificial face and prowled about with his true face, so as not to be recognized!"

Moon-face stood up, nodded slowly. "I guess that's all, Miss Sibley. We may need you again later, but that's all for now."

Abel Gravlin, Mariah, and their halfwit son stared as Cary Booth put an arm around the girl and steered her to the door. Quentin Planchard stared, too. Outside, the village square was a quagmire; rain had ceased falling from a sky of scurrying clouds.

Irma Sibley's fingers tightened on Cary's arm and the girl said anxiously: "You—you'll walk home with me?"

He held her arm closely. They tramped slowly through wet grass beside the road. "John hated you, didn't he?" he said.

"With me out of the way," she answered wearily, "he could have had all dad's money. When he found me prowling about the inn last night, he dragged me to that awful room and chloroformed me and— Oh, Cary, it's horrible! He hated me and—and he must have known that I suspected him!"

"Why were you prowling around the inn?"

"Because you were a prisoner there. I wanted to help, if I could. And I came back again, after father's death, because John's actions were so queer. He was so anxious to be rid of me—"

"He wanted to get back in a hurry," Cary said, "for his robe and the rest of his monster equipment, before someone else found them. There would be fingerprints on the handcuff-keys in the robe's pocket, and—" His arm tightened about her, held her more closely to him. Ahead, gray clouds parted in a gray sky and sunlight slanted down, changing the wet grass to an aisle of gleaming gold.

"I thought at first," Cary said, "that Redfern was the man behind the mask. But even then I knew better. Redfern was ill with a disease that caused him to wander about in agony. He didn't commit that first murder. He wandered into the wrong room in the dark, and when he heard the woman scream in the adjoining room it frightened him. The blood on his hands and face was his own. Terror brought on a hemorrhage."

The Sibley home loomed ahead, strangely white and clean through sun-streaked mist. But Cary kept on talking. There were things on his mind that he wanted to spill out and then forget.

"I knew they were wrong about your father. When I fought him and stripped the artificial flesh from one of his hands, I saw the twisted stump beneath. In the torture-room, when I fought the monster, I saw his hand and it was normal."

"But why did John want to kill you and me—that way?"

"The more horrible the method, the better it fitted with his plans. He had painted your father as a madman; the murders had to fit in with that. So did the black robe, the phosphorescent eyes, the mask and all the rest of it. He wanted you out of the way so he could have all your father's money, and he had to get rid of me because the police were ready to accept me as the killer. That would have spoiled everything. John tried to keep them from capturing me, and failed, and then had to commit another murder of which I could *not* be guilty. Don't you see?"

But Irma Sibley was seeing something else. Ahead of her, on the sun-tinted bough of a white birch, an orange-breasted oriole was trilling notes of happiness. The girl's hand found Cary's and clung there. "Look!" she whispered. "Look! Isn't he lovely?"

A trace of hysteria was in her voice, but Cary Booth looked into her face and knew that the hysteria would soon be gone, and the voice would be as soft, as sweet as the lips that uttered it.

Before very long there would be other orioles. He and she would see them, together, and both would laugh and be happy. And black memories would be forgotten....

THE END

HUGH B. CAVE

DARK BONDAGE

The curse of old Benjamin Merritt was upon Milton Perry, blighting all that he touched, sending those he loved to agony and death....

*I*T WAS, for Fiskeville, an event as important as the signing of the Declaration of Independence. When the last pen had scratched out the signature of its wielder, the murmuring drone of voices in the crowded courtroom became an undulating tidal wave of sound. Fiskeville's citizens surged forward and would have carried Milton Perry in triumph through the tree-lined streets of that peaceful New England town, had not Perry grinned quietly and pushed them away.

Yet the smile on Perry's lips was slightly grim as he walked with the town's selectmen and Martin Gregg, manufacturer's representative, through the ranks of patriotic citizens who cheered his name. For at the rear of the room, near the door, stood a small group of townspeople who were not cheering—who were, instead, glowering at him as if he were something unclean that had defiled the air they breathed.

With a hand on Perry's arm, Martin Gregg said lightly, "Well, young fellow, I guess you've won. Won a clear victory. It won't be long before that handful of conservatives will get over their superstitious objections and be glad you made 'em come to terms!"

Perry's answering smile was forced. Glancing into the pinched, sallow face of Anton Walzek, emissary of the rival company whose bid had been turned down by the committee, he saw hatred in it, and a veiled threat. And as he neared the threshold he glanced again at his defeated foes, and stopped. Then and there, he would have begged for the hundredth time that they bury the hatchet and try to understand his motives in bringing a factory to the town which had always been his home and to which he had pledged his allegiance. But Everett Latham, beside him, nudged him forward.

"Not now, Perry," Latham said wisely. "Better wait until they've cooled off."

Then, as Perry stepped into the corridor, pent-up hatred burst its dam.

Old Benjamin Merritt was the man who lurched forward. Old Merritt, who only half an hour ago had faced the crowded meeting and croaked out, with half-mad vehemence, that he would never, while still alive and able to fight, permit Fiskeville's most sacred shrine to be defiled by factory buildings. Old Merritt, whose ancestors had fought beside Benjamin Church in the conquest of King Philip and the Wampanoags—whose forefathers had brandished muskets against Gage at Bunker Hill.

Fists clenched, bloodshot eyes glowing with fanatical rage that had broken its bonds, old Merritt stumbled from the little knot of discontented townsmen near the door. Lurching forward, he shrilled words that brought Milton Perry to a halt.

"Wait a minute—you! I got somethin' to say to you!"

The blood of fighting ancestors fumed in Benjamin Merritt's emaciated frame. Like a huge crab, clawing hands outflung, he surged through the gaping crowd and planted himself on trembling legs before Perry. His grey-haired head was cocked sideways; his smouldering eyes were live coals in a withered face whose muscles worked convulsively.

"You listen to me, Milton Perry! You listen to what I say and mark my words! No man alive can do what you're proposin' to do and escape judgment for his sins! You hear me?"

Perry sighed, said softly: "I hear you, Merritt." Compassion gripped him. It was impossible not to admire the courage of this wizened old man who was still at heart a colonist and dwelt mentally in times long past. Old Merritt was not to blame for this savage outburst. More than likely the scheme had been spawned in the cunning mind of Ora Fiske, leader of the anti-factory delegation.

But Merritt's clawing fingers raked aside the hand that Perry extended to calm him. "I'm warnin' you, Milton Perry! If you destroy the sanctity of Jason's Knoll by puttin' up a factory there, you'll pay for it! It's blasphemy against Almighty God! You put up your factory on hallowed ground, and the curse of God goes with it!"

Perry was silent as were the amazed people around him. In the doorway stood Ora Fiske and the rest of Merritt's companions, grimly staring. Off to one side stood Anthony Walzek, the defeated factory-representative whose bid had been refused. The victorious murmur of the townspeople no longer filled the corridor. Merritt's shrill voice was the only sound in a sudden, unnatural hush.

"My curse be on you, Milton Perry! The curse of Benjamin Merritt, whose ancestors helped to hang the Salem witches! The breath of doom on you! Mad am I? Mad or not, I tell you you'll pay! You'll bring death and doom to everyone and everything you love! You'll bring disaster on everyone you put a hand on and everyone you try to help! That's what comes to a black-souled fiend who defiles the shrine of—"

The old man retched backward, his face livid. His hands ceased clawing at Perry's clothes and went to his own throat, fingers curled in sudden agony. Foam flecked his thin lips and whitened his yellow teeth. Surging blood made a carmine gargoyle of his face.

Perry jerked forward, eyes wide with sudden apprehension. But old Benjamin Merritt went down, writhing. On the floor he screamed:

"My curse on you! The curse of me and my ancestors, who hanged the Salem witches! Mad, am I? Mad I may be, but *not half as mad as you'll be*—"

Perry's hands clutched the old man's body and raised it, despite its writhing and twisting. The amazed spectators opened a path as he carried the stricken man over the threshold into the courtroom. Like a siren, Merritt's voice shrieked through the strange hush.

"Take your filthy hands off me, Milton Perry! Take 'em away! They're death hands and the curse is on them! Don't be touchin' me!"

Perry lowered him to a bench, straightened above that writhing figure and looked desperately into the faces around him. "Get a doctor, one of you! Hurry!"

"Death hands!" Merritt screamed. "Hands o' death, and they touched me! A doctor can't do no good now! It's too late. Too late...."

The scream expired in a bloody gurgle. Benjamin Merritt's bony hands ceased clawing at the wooden bench; his wizened body stiffened with a convulsive jerk. With horrified eyes Perry stared down at him.

The old man's bulging orbs were no longer on fire with smouldering passion. They were sightless glass marbles coated with film. Just once the matchstick legs twitched, and the foam-flecked mouth released a low moan as of wind sighing through wet leaves.

Then old Benjamin Merritt was dead.

GREY haired Hallam Jordon hunched forward in a rocker on the front porch of the Jordon home on Main Street, and blinked up into Perry's pale face. "Good Lord, Perry," he said, "don't take it so hard! First thing you know, you'll be broodin' yourself into thinking the old man's curse has something in it. Don't be a fool! Benjamin Merritt died of heart-attack and nothing else. He had one foot in the grave anyway."

Perry forced a weak smile and looked down at himself. Hallam Jordon was right, of course. Yet even Jordon's blunt words were insufficient to drive away the feeling of uneasiness that had festered for hours in his mind.

He didn't fear old Merritt's curse. It wasn't that. Probably he was just tired out, after days and weeks of fighting for what he knew to be right. From the very beginning, a certain few inhabitants of Fiskeville had fought tooth and nail against the prospect of securing for the town a factory which would practically solve its unemployment problem. They were wrong in fighting against it! Dead wrong! Such a factory would mean better business for everyone concerned, and would increase by some thousands of dollars the money spent in the town.

Yet Ora Fiske and Merritt and a few others had accused him of scheming to make a fortune for himself at the expense of the town's good reputation. They should know better than that. He had lived in Fiskeville all his twenty-six years, had fought to build the very reputation they now accused him of scheming to tear down. And—he was engaged to wed Janice Jordon, the daughter of Sarah and Hallam Jordon, who were staunch loyalists and firm New England Yankees.

What more proof of his allegiance could Ora Fiske and the others demand?

Yet he understood their motives. Fiskeville, because of its limited railroad facilities, had possessed only one site acceptable to the mammoth textile corporation which had agreed to give the town a factory. That site had once been something of a shrine. Neglected and weed-grown now, it was nevertheless cloaked in deep-rooted sentiment.

"You can't build on hallowed ground!" Ora Fiske had thundered at the meeting. "Jason's Knoll is sacred to the memories of what happened there! Maybe your people didn't make it sacred, but ours did!"

Yes, Jason's Knoll was a hallowed ground, if one believed in legends that had been handed down through the years. On Jason's Knoll a band of early settlers, fighting for their lives against red-skinned fiends led by King Philip himself, had prayed for divine aid and received it. Besieged by painted savages, the handful of whites had turned to a priestly one of their number—and that man, if legends did not lie, had fallen to his knees in a pool of his own ebbing lifeblood, and prayed as only a devout Puritan could pray. And in the deepest hour of darkness had come a miracle—blinding sheets of rain, livid shafts of white lightning in a furious storm which had spiked the hearts of King Philip's warriors with terror, causing them to flee.

Many years later, on that same hallowed ground, a valiant band of Americans had again prayed for divine aid when menaced by British troops. Their leader, Randall Fiske—whose blood now flowed in the veins of Ora Fiske—had knelt and prayed in the face of withering musket-fire, then had arisen in glory, and with heaven-sent inspiration led his doomed band to miraculous victory.

Hallowed ground? Yes. But since the days of Lincoln and the Civil War, Jason's Knoll had lived less and less in the memories of the townspeople; and now only a few pseudo-sentimental zealots, aroused by Ora Fiske and Benjamin Merritt, opposed the plan of turning that weed-grown site into a commercial enterprise which would raise Fiskeville from debt and despair.

Nevertheless, Milton Perry stared anxiously at the grey-haired man who scowled up at him. "It isn't that I fear old Merritt's curse, Mr. Jordon. I don't. But Merritt's death will make Ora Fiske and the others even more determined in their opposition. They'll see in it a recurrence of that divine intervention they've been prating about. They'll call it a work of God and a warning."

"Nonsense, boy!"

"But they will! You don't know them!"

"I know them better than you do." Hallam Jordon's deep eyes narrowed in wrinkled flesh-pits. "I know enough about 'em, my boy, to be scared of old Merritt's curse if I were superstitious that way, which I'm not. The history books say that some of Benjamin Merritt's ancestors were burned at the stake for practicing arts forbidden by Almighty God. But the books don't tell the whole story. I've looked into those things and I know more than you do. Go ahead with your plans and don't be afraid. No future son-in-law of mine can back down because of an old man's curse!"

Perry nodded slowly. "I'll stick it out, Mr. Jordon. Come hell or high water, I'll stick."

"Good! And when Janice gets back from her visit to the city, she'll be right smart proud of you!"

Perry smiled, felt a warm glow creep inside him, driving out the chill that had taken possession of his heart. The sound of Hallam Jordon's blustering voice was soothing; that voice was real and honest, not in the least like the screeching howl of old Benjamin Merritt.

Afraid of Merritt's curse? Not he! Merritt had been queer anyway; perhaps even half mad.

He felt better as he hiked down the steps and opened the gate. Behind him, Hallam Jordon leaned back in the rocker and smiled knowingly; and if the smile were of short duration, changing to a doubtful shake of the head and a squint-eyed frown, Perry did not turn to see.

ALL the way home, he pondered Hallam Jordon's advice. Home was a small white cottage on the outskirts of town: a cozy dwelling where Milton Perry had lived alone for nearly four years. Right now, it looked more friendly than ever. Here there would be no thoughts of old Merritt's grisly curse, or of the veiled threat in Anthony Walzek's thin face, or of Ora Fiske and his muttering cohorts.

He walked slowly up the flagstoned path and glanced with pride at the beds of varicolored flowers blooming near the veranda. They at least understood him and did not doubt his allegiance. They did not curse him.

Inside, he stripped to his shirtsleeves, donned slippers and lounging-robe, and prepared to make supper. On occasions the townspeople had thought him queer for living alone. A rising young manufacturer, ambitious and progressive, living by himself in a small white cottage, with only flowers for company? Incredible! They did not know that he spent weary hours hunched over a kitchen table cluttered with plans and blueprints; they should have known that his love for flowers was inherited from the grey-haired mother who had died four years ago in this same white cottage.

Janice, too, loved flowers. In a little while, not longer than a few weeks, this white cottage would be hers; these lonely rooms would awaken to the sweet murmur of her voice.

The thought warmed Perry's heart-blood. Then another thought, that of old Merritt's vicious curse, returned to supplant it. He shuddered and stood rigid, staring into shadows.

The thought persisted, intensifying the cold chill in his soul, until the white cottage was no longer a place of peace and quiet. In the very thud of his own footsteps Perry heard other steps that were not real and yet were terrifyingly relentless. In the soft whistle of the kettle on the stove another sound was born: a vague, faint mockery of Benjamin Merritt's shrieking voice screaming words of madness.

And while Perry sat at the kitchen table, listlessly stuffing food between pale lips, the gnarled face of old Merritt took form in deepening shadows and hung like a gaunt leering gargoyle always beyond reach.

But that was madness! Only a fool would believe such things! Thrusting the food away from him, Perry lurched erect, stood trembling in every muscle, his hands white and tense on the table top. Words snarled through the room and they were his own. "What am I, anyway? A five-year-old kid scared of the dark? For God's sake, snap out of it!"

He laughed then, but the laugh was empty of humor. Later, when he paced nervously into the living-room, the face of old Merritt went with him and Merritt's raucous voice was in that room, too. No, not in the room. The voice was in his brain, where he could not smother it or escape it.

He went to a mammoth window-box choked with flowers—a box of red and gold glowing in lamplight—and watered them. He spent the best part of half an hour tending them; but even their soft beauty could not stifle the misgiving in his heart. No matter where his steps took him or what his hands were doing, old Merritt's voice screamed in his soul.

"The breath of doom on you, Milton Perry! Doom to everyone and everything you love!"

And again: *"Death hands! Hands o' death and they touched me! A doctor can't do no good now! It's too late...."*

Hours later, when he climbed the stairs to the small white-walled bedroom and threw himself on the bed, cold sweat beaded his twitching face and his eyes were blood-rimmed from staring so long into shadows. He lay rigid, gazing dully at the ceiling. And he thought: This is madness! These hands of mine had nothing to do with old Merritt's death! Good God, what am I—a coward? Am I fool enough to let the death of one old man, who was half mad and would have died anyway, make a gibbering scarecrow of me?

He slept, but the sleep was filled with leering shadows and a gaunt face screaming words of evil. Nightmares tormented him in endless procession. Old Merritt came, and Ora Fiske, and a handful of muttering townspeople who threatened dire things. And in his dream he ran screaming in terror to the home of Hallam Jordon, where Janice held her arms out to him and comforted him and said softly: "What are you afraid of?"

Morning came and the sheets of the bed were damp with perspiration. Exhausted by a sleep which had been no sleep at all, Perry went downstairs, made a breakfast for which he had no appetite. This day there was work to be done. He must visit Jason's Knoll and talk with Martin Gregg, the manufacturer's representative who would supervise the work of construction. And yet he was tired....

Wearily he walked into the living-room and took his hat and coat from a chair. And then, looking toward the flower-box over which he had worked so painstakingly the night before, he stiffened abruptly, opened his eyes wide.

A sob welled in his throat as he lurched forward. He put both hands out, and the fingers of those hands were ice cold and twitching when they touched the rim of the flower-box.

The flowers were no longer beautiful, no longer a vivid sea of color. They were withered, drooping mockeries of a loveliness that had faded. It was as if years instead of hours had passed during the night, as if some malignant malady had brought death. For the flowers in that box—the same blooms over which he had worked with such care and tenderness—were seared and ugly. Black emblems of death!

Milton Perry stared with widening, glazed eyes at the stiff fingers of his ice-cold hands, and shrieked hysterically: *"Death hands! Oh my God...."*

CHAPTER TWO

OUT OF THE GRAVE

WHAT HAPPENED immediately after that, he was not sure. For an eternity, terror had him in its relentless grip. He stumbled backward and slumped like a drunken man into one of the room's many chairs.

Fear of madness spiked him. He gripped the chair-arms fiercely and fought for self-control. Over and over he mumbled aloud: "It wasn't the curse! It *wasn't!* Such things can't be true...."

The thing that saved him, finally bringing self-control, was a sudden realization that the phone was ringing. The sound stiffened him, droned through the hoarse words of horror that spilled from his throat. He crossed the threshold and snatched the instrument in trembling fingers.

Over the wire came a harsh masculine voice that blasted his eardrums.

"Perry? This is Latham. Perry, in God's name come over here! I'm at Hallam Jordon's house. Something terrible—"

The voice broke in a sob. The phone slipped from Perry's stiff fingers and for seconds he stood staring at it. Everett Latham—at the Jordon home? A green glint of jealousy gathered in Perry's eyes. What was Latham doing there?

He had no great liking for the man, even though he had taken him into the newly formed textile corporation. But there was nothing really wrong with Latham. He was Jan's second cousin and held a good position in the Fiskeville Bank, of which Hallam Jordon was owner. A good man and an honest one. But—he had long been a rival for the hand of Hallam Jordon's daughter. He had wanted Janice....

Then, dully, Perry realized what the voice had said. The Jordon home. Something terrible....

Good God, if anything had happened to Janice!

It was a quarter-mile to the Jordon home, and Milton Perry had his car out of its small white garage and over that quarter-mile of rutted road in less than five minutes. Janice Jordon's father was not this time sitting on the trellised porch. It was Everett Latham who jerked the door open when Perry pushed the bell.

And the face of Janice Jordon's cousin was no longer normal and handsome. It was a chalk-hued mask racked with torment. The hand that stabbed out to grip Perry's arm was quivering as with ague.

"Thank God you've come, Perry! I couldn't have handled this alone. Mrs. Jordon is on the verge of hysterics—"

"What's wrong?" Fear whitened Perry's lips. "Is it Jan? Has anything—"

"It's not Jan. It's Hallam! The sheriff has been here." Latham shuddered. "There's been a murder and they've taken Hallam. Taken him to jail. They say he killed Martin Gregg!"

Perry heard sobbing sounds from the living-room and lurched forward, forced his leaden legs to carry him over the threshold. At his entrance the wife of Hallam Jordon raised her bowed head and looked up at him. Sobs shook her thin shoulders; her body, slender despite its burden of years, was a small, trembling thing huddled in a chair that seemed enormous by comparison. Her white hands gripped the chair-arms. Her face was racked with anguish under its halo of grey-white hair.

Perry went to her and put an arm about her shoulders. The anguish in her bloodless face found its way into his own heart. "Don't, Mrs. Jordon! Please don't. It isn't as bad as that. It—can't be. There's a horrible mistake."

"She won't be comforted," Latham groaned. "God knows I've tried. I hurried here as soon as I learned what had happened. It *must* be a mistake! But the sheriff found what he said was damning evidence—"

"Found—what?"

"Evidence." Latham's voice bubbled through moist lips. "He and his men searched the house. They had a man's boot-heel—the double-thick heel—that Hallam always wears. They said it was found on the hotel fire-escape, outside the room where Gregg was shot. They went through the house here as if they owned it, and they found one of Hallam's shoes in a closet upstairs, with the heel ripped off. They took him—"

He clenched his fists, glared at Perry with eyes that suddenly smouldered. "It's a dirty frameup, Perry. Ora Fiske and Walzek are back of it! At the meeting yesterday, when old Merritt pulled his little act, Fiske and Walzek were mumbling together as if guilty of something underhanded. If ever I saw a look of fiendish delight on a man's face, it was on Walzek's. By God—"

He stared at Sarah Jordon and suddenly stopped talking. A shuddering moan had escaped the woman's lips: her head was on Perry's shoulder. But she said nothing. Torment had robbed her of speech.

Compassion filled Perry's heart and he tightened his arms about those slender shoulders. "It's a mistake, Mrs. Jordon," he whispered again. "It's nothing more than that. You must be brave."

The woman stared up at him. "Oh God, it isn't true! Tell them it isn't true!"

"I'll go to them now. And I'll bring him back with me. I promise!" Perry withdrew his arm and stood up, caught a deep breath.

"Take care of her, Latham," he muttered. Then, bitterly: "I won't be long. I'll make them listen to reason."

HE strode savagely from the house and hiked downtown with long ground-eating strides. Hallam Jordon a murderer? Did the sheriff and the rest of them believe even for a moment in a thing so utterly impossible? What if they had found "evidence"? Evidence could be faked or framed or invented, but a man's character could not change overnight! They should know that....

If murder had been done, and evidence planted, the ghastly deed was but another part of the vicious program of terror sponsored by Ora Fiske and his fanatic followers. Another savage attempt to prevent what they, in their blind madness, chose to call the desecration of Jason's Knoll!

Would they stop at nothing?

Outside the courthouse jail a crowd had formed, and Perry pushed his way through with savage strides. Inside, he came upon another group and found himself confronting Ora Fiske, Sheriff Andrew Gates, and other Fiskeville citizens.

Fiske, sitting pompously in a swivelchair before the desk, was speaking in a high-pitched womanish voice that harmonized with his watery grey eyes, bony frame, and bilious face.

"That's exactly what happened, I'm telling you. I went to the hotel this morning to make a last attempt to persuade Gregg to abandon his plans. Henry Johnson, the clerk, was at the lobby desk when I went upstairs. I went up alone and knocked on Gregg's door—number twenty-three as I recall it—and there wasn't no answer. And then I saw a dark stain on the floor, right at my feet."

Fiske screwed his pink lips out of shape and jerked his head to spit at a cuspidor beside the desk. "That dark stain was blood, and it come from under Gregg's door. So I hustled downstairs and got Johnson, and we opened the door, and there was Gregg layin' on the floor, just over the sill. He'd been shot sometime durin' the night and he'd been shot in the back. The window was open overlookin' the fire-escape. It's plain as the nose on your face what happened."

Sheriff Gates nodded, reached down to pick up a shoe that stood on the desk. Perry, moving forward, said quietly, "May I look at that, Sheriff?"

But a close look was not necessary. Beside the shoe lay the torn heel that obviously belonged to it. Only one man in Fiskeville wore a double-thick leather heel of that type. Hallam Jordon had been forced to suffer such a contrivance since childhood, when infantile paralysis had left its mark.

"I reckon it's open and shut," Gates said grimly. "We found the heel on the hotel fire-escape outside Gregg's window. Soon as we examined it, we knew who it belonged to. What reason

Jordon had for wantin' to kill Gregg, we ain't yet been able to figure out—and Jordon won't talk. But it's apparent he done the shootin', and in makin' his getaway he got his heel caught in one of the rusty iron slats of the fire escape."

"And then?" Perry's prompting came in a whisper through twitching lips.

"Well, we naturally went to Jordon's house and accused him, and when he denied knowin' anything about it we searched the house. We located the shoe, with the heel ripped off of it, in a cupboard up in an unused bedroom. He swore up and down that he ain't worn that particular pair of shoes in six months or more, but—well, evidence don't lie."

Perry's hand closed tremblingly on the sheriff's arm. "Let me talk to Hallam."

"Why sure, if you want to." Gates swung about, pushed through the crowded room and led the way along the jail corridor, rattling keys in his outthrust hand. At the corridor's end he stopped, opened a cell-door and nodded. "I'll have to lock you in, Mr. Perry. Holler when you're done talkin', and I'll come let you out again."

Perry stepped forward, shuddered as the door rattled shut behind him. Then he was alone with the man who sat staring at him.

The cell was small, and sunlight slanted through a barred window close to the ceiling. Hallam Jordon sat in shadow, on a cot that sagged under the weight of his big body—sat and stared, with deep eyes glowering in sunken sockets. Beside him, on the floor, dirty dishes were stacked against the wall. A cigarette protruded at a defiant upward angle from his tight lips, and grey smoke hung without motion in the narrow room.

Perry moved forward, said falteringly: "Mr. Jordon...."

The dark eyes narrowed; the thin lips curled downward. "Well, Perry?"

"They're mad out there! Stark mad, all of them! Ora Fiske has egged them on with his fanatic ravings, and all they can think of is Fiske and Merritt and Merritt's curse."

HE stopped abruptly, stood stiff. In the anguish of the past half hour he had forgotten the hideous words of Benjamin Merritt. Now he remembered, and the muscles of his throat contracted with sudden chill. Those dead flowers. "You'll bring death and doom to *everyone you try to help!*" Great God....

"It makes no difference what they think now," Hallam Jordon said bitterly. "They've branded me. They've called me a killer and thrown me in prison. That's all that matters. My wife and daughter are shamed forever."

Perry took a faltering step forward. It was no time now to think of Merritt's curse. Such thoughts were madness. Old Merritt had died; the flowers had rotted away—but not because of any wild threat flung from the heart of a half-mad lunatic! Hallam Jordon needed help. Needed it now!

His hand gripped the older man's shoulder. "Your wife and daughter are not shamed. The whole thing is a foolish mistake, that's all."

But he knew now that the murder of Martin Gregg had been no mistake. Gregg had been slain because of his determination to see the Jason's Knoll deal through, despite all opposition. He had been shot down because he represented the company that was backing Perry's plans.

But why had the unknown killer elected to plant evidence that would convict Hallam Jordon?

Jordon owned the Fiskeville Trust Company. Perhaps....

"Son—" Jordon's hand trembled on Perry's rigid arm. "Son, I've a feeling I'm not coming out of this. It's the end. Take care of Janice and—"

A girl's voice from the jail corridor outside interrupted him. He stiffened, stared with widening eyes at the cell door. Perry's eyes widened, too, and filled with gladness. He knew that voice! Since Jan had left Fiskeville, two weeks ago, and gone to visit friends in a nearby city, he had missed that voice and its owner as much as a man could miss anything on earth.

He lurched erect, strode to the cell door and stared past the stocky form of Sheriff Gates into the anxious face of the girl he loved. Then the door creaked open and Janice Jordon was in his arms.

She clung to him only a moment, then turned impulsively, put both arms around the rigid body of her father and stared with wide moist eyes into Hallam's gaunt face.

In the past moment that face had changed! Color had seeped out of it and left a bloodless mask. Jordon's eyes were glowing live coals; the flesh of his cheeks was sucked in, like thin rubber, over bulging muscles that worked convulsively! Spittle flecked the man's lips and he gasped for breath as if suffocating.

"It—it's too late, girl. Too—late...."

Too late! Perry stared in horror as that husky voice whispered through the room. It was not Jordon's voice; it was the muttered croak of old Benjamin Merritt, wheezing the same ominous words. "Too—late...."

Moments ago, Hallam Jordon had been physically well. Now the man was a gaunt, trembling scarecrow, sick unto death!

Death hands! A chill of horror stabbed Perry's heart. Slowly, against his will, he raised his own two hands and stared at them. Was it his mad imagination, or did those lean fingers curl toward his gaping eyes, of their own volition, in a gesture of black mockery? Death hands! Merciful God...!

Hallam Jordon's hoarse voice broke through the shroud of midnight fear that enveloped him. "I'm done for, girl. Done for."

"But what's *wrong*, Dad? Oh God, tell me what's wrong!"

"I don't know." Hallam's voice came weakly. "Light me a cigarette, Jan, like a good—girl. I don't know what's wrong. It came of a sudden. I—I'm choked up—can't breathe." He raised his head as if it were weighted, and his palsied hand came up to take the cigarette the girl offered him. His glazed eyes focused, as if gazing through dense fog, on Perry's rigid form.

"Merritt's—curse." The words came half inaudibly, struggling through weak lips. "There must be something—to it—after all. I was all right till Perry came in here. Then—he put his hands on me...."

Blood rushed to Jordon's gaunt face. Suddenly he was erect on widespread legs, swaying. His lips worked furiously, spitting grey froth, and he stood like a blasted tower ready to crash. His arm jerked up a lean forefinger stabbed toward Perry's wooden form.

"You leave my daughter alone! God help you—"

His big body pitched forward and the girl's clutching hands could not hold him. Foaming at the mouth, he crashed to the floor and lay still.

PERRY did not move. He could not move. The blood in his veins had congealed; his rigid frame was ice-cold, stiff as stone. He stood with both hands half extended, eyes bulging and filled with black terror. And Janice Jordon, even while kneeling beside the fallen body of her father and sobbing incoherent words of anguish, stared at Perry as if gazing at a specter from some dark room of hell.

"Is he—is he dead?" Perry whispered.

She shuddered, made no answer. Slowly he took a step forward, but her shrill voice blasted out to stop him. "Don't come near me! Don't touch him! My God, haven't you done enough *already?*"

Perry closed his eyes in agony. So she, too, had heard about old Merritt's mad curse. Even though she had but just returned to Fiskeville, she had heard the whole ghastly story and believed it.

He groaned, retreated step by step from the girl's wild gaze. Of course she had heard. A score of gossiping tongues would have poured the hideous story into her ears. And now, now she had witnessed the horrific power of the curse that damned him. She had seen with her own eyes....

Vaguely, through a mental agony that numbed him, he was aware of other voices, other shapes crowding around him. The cell door was open; Sheriff Gates was in the room, gaping down at Hallam Jordon's contorted body. Others were gawking in the doorway, pushing closer.

But their stares of astonishment changed rapidly to something else. Their attention went from the dead man to the man who stood stiff and pale in their midst. With one accord they shrank from him, gazed at him in terror.

Ora Fiske, peering into Perry's face, cringed back and muttered aloud: "It's the curse of old Merritt. 'The breath o' doom,' Merritt said, and it's true. First he died, and now Jordon!"

A moan of mortal anguish welled in Perry's throat; he took a step forward, arms outstretched toward the girl who had loved him. "It isn't true! Oh God, it can't be. Jan—"

The horror in her wide eyes stopped him. For a moment he stood rooted to the floor while his gaze roved dully from one fear-filled face to another. Then panic seized him; he stumbled blindly to the door. They let him go, shrank from him as from a leper.

With madness in his heart, Perry lurched through the jail corridor and out of the building. And outside, where the news of Jordon's death and the manner of it had circulated through the assembled crowd, men and women fell back in wide-eyed horror to let him through.

Alone, he returned to the small white cottage on the outskirts of the town. He made his way into a bleak living-room where dead flowers leered at him from the window-box. Sitting there in a chair near the black fireplace, he stared with hollow, vacant eyes—and saw only the leering face of old Merritt, heard only the shrill cacophony of Merritt's voice screaming, as from a great distance:

"The breath of doom on you, Milton Perry! Death and doom to everyone you love...."

The breath of doom! How long that soul-retching thought endured in Perry's mind, he did not know. Hours passed before other thoughts came to supplant it.

What had become of Sarah Jordon? Had the shock been too much for her? Had Latham stayed with her, to comfort her?

Slowly, Perry got out of his chair and went to the telephone, forced himself to raise the receiver from its hook and call the Jordon home.

Everett Latham answered, and said quietly in reply to Perry's mumbled questions: "She is under the doctor's care. The shock was great, but she has a good chance to pull through, thank God. How about you?"

"I'm—all right."

"I want to talk to you, Perry. No, I'm not afraid of the curse. It may be some time before I'm able to leave here, but I'll come as soon as possible. Janice is still at the jail, with Sheriff Gates and the others."

Perry hooked the receiver, returned to the living-room. For a while he stared at his hands, and shuddered. Then he forced himself to stop shuddering. Death hands? After what had happened, it was easy to believe that Merritt's curse had given those lean fingers the power to destroy whatever they contacted. But such things could not be! This was the twentieth century, not a dark age of sorcery and witchcraft!

Someone, someone with sinister designs, was behind all this. But who? Ora Fiske? One of Fiske's fanatical followers? Or Anthony Walzek, the man who had tried to get the factory site for his own company?

Or even Sheriff Gates, who had long been a close friend of Fiske and might now be in league with those same fanatics?

Benjamin Merritt was dead. The flowers in the window-box were black mockeries. Hallam Jordon was dead. How could Fiske or Gates or Walzek or any other one man have been responsible for such a hideous sequence of events?

Perry sat and thought, until he found himself unable to think. A dull longing stabbed his heart. His arms went slowly out; the name of the girl he loved came convulsively from his pale lips. Then he remembered the horror in Janice Jordon's eyes when she had cringed from him in her father's death-cell, and he uttered a low groan of torment that came from the depths of a soul dark with agony.

Even *she* believed that a black curse hung over him threatening doom to all he loved!

He stood up, gaunt and trembling, and paced slowly into the kitchen. While coffee was brewing on the stove, he stood before a mirror and gazed at his reflection in the glass. The face he saw was no longer his own. It was a strange, uncouth gargoyle with sunken eyes and hollow cheeks. Madness hung in the terror-glare of its eyes. Leprous white, frightful in its paleness, it glared back at him so fiercely that he shrank from it.

HE had no desire for coffee then, or for food. Silently he returned to the living-room. Hours had passed since his return to the cottage, and when he drew the window curtains aside now and peered out at the street, he saw that it lay in darkness. Night had come. Creeping shadows filled the room, and the shadows brought a new fear, a new dread.

Alone and lonely, Perry sank into a chair, lighted a small lamp on the table beside him. Damp hair hung in his staring eyes. He had long ago discarded coat and tie and exchanged his shoes for slippers. Lamplight cast wriggling shadows over him, yellowing his face and hands. In the silence of creeping night, the house became a thing alive and acquired a voice. Not one voice, but many. And at every vague sound, Perry jerked to attention, sat like a stone image while his wide eyes sought an explanation.

In the room with him, a clock ticked the passing seconds. Strange, the human quality in that sound, as of some skeleton finger gently but relentlessly tapping out seconds of doom. It came from behind him, throbbing into his brain, repeating the same word over and over without pause or variation. *Doom... doom... doom... doom....*

Then it was no longer a whisper, but the shrill voice of old Merritt, screaming forth in savage glee its ominous message. DOOM! DOOM! DOOM! How in the name of God could any voice go on and on, on and on like that without pausing for breath? How—

Perry lurched erect and his own voice shrieked an answer. "In God's name, stop it! *Stop it!*"

Like a blind man he lurched across the room, stumbling, crashing against chairs and tables, his arms outflung, his hands clawing like twin crabs. The offending clock squatted on a mantel near the hall doorway, leering at him. His fingers seized it, curled around it. With a hoarse cry of triumph he flung the clock from him, heard it crash against the wall and thud to the floor. The voice of old Merritt died to silence.

He realized then what he had done. Cold sweat broke out on his forehead and he stood rigid. Whispered words spilled from his lips. "My God—am I going *mad?*"

There was no answer. Slowly, with groping hands outstretched, he returned to the chair. Mad? Yes. None but a madman would have let the harmless ticking of a clock affect him that way. A hoarse sob rose in his throat, found utterance in a ghastly moan of fear. Then another sound found its way into the room and worked on his diseased nerves.

Behind him, the windows rattled to a sudden sharp impact, as a wind-driven gust of rain drummed against them. The house had possessed whispering ghost-voices before, but now it became an abode of inhuman din. The drumming of heavy rain was a devil's tattoo throbbing in his brain....

He listened, and felt hair crawl at the nape of his neck. The beat of his heart quickened as his warped imagination played tricks with him. That sudden whispering sound above him—was it a stealthy tread of feet in an upstairs room, or merely an echo of rain on the sloping roof? That demon laughter from the kitchen—was it something more than the wail of wind against creaking windows?

Out in the hall a clock was striking, and the sound was a beating of huge hammers against Perry's twisted brain. *Bong... bong... bong....* Merciful Christ, would it never cease? Yet he counted the strokes, widened his eyes in bewilderment as they continued. Ten... eleven.... It could not be that late! Twelve! The huge clock was silent. Twelve o'clock! Midnight! No, no—!

But he knew it was true. For hours he had lived in torment, enduring the tortures of the damned. Time had meant nothing. Now it was midnight!

He moaned dully. Everett Latham would not come now. Latham had thought things over and realized the horrible truth and decided to stay away. No one would ever come again.

Perry stiffened in his chair. A sound not of the storm had found its way into the room. Seconds passed while he clung to the chair-arms, his body twisted half about, his red-rimmed eyes focused on the hall doorway. Yes, there it was again. A thud of heavy feet on the veranda steps, outside. Latham had come!

With a glad cry he heaved himself erect, stumbled into the hall. Even before the door echoed to the dull thud of a pounding fist he was lurching toward it, his hand outflung to grip the knob.

Then, as the knob burned hot against his icy fingers, he hesitated, sucked breath into his heaving chest.

What if it were not Latham? What if it were someone—something else—some monstrous visitant conjured up by old Merritt's black curse?

The thought knifed his brain and spawned a sob in his throat. What matter now if the vilest demons of hell came to claim him! Death would be better than creeping madness. Anything would be better than living in a dark world of eternal terror!

In a low, trembling voice he called out: "Who—who's there?"

No voice answered him. Again the door vibrated to the impact of a thumping fist.

"*Who's there?*" Perry shrieked. "*Who is it?*"

Did a voice answer him? He was not sure. Faintly, through the throb of heavy rain and the moan of storm-wind in the upper reaches of the house, a low voice seemed to intone: "Open—and see." Was his brain again playing tricks?…

Slowly his fingers turned the knob. It would not be Latham. Latham would have thumbed the bell instead of knocking. It was some stranger….

Then the door was open. With horror-filled eyes Perry stared into the dark, drooling face of the man who stood on the veranda.

Rain puddled the porch and cascaded from the eaves above. Rain and darkness blurred the hunch-shouldered shape that stood just beyond the open door. But the face that glared at Perry from beneath the down-turned brim of a sodden black hat *was the face of Benjamin Merritt!*

CHAPTER THREE

The Curse Falls

A SCREAM GURGLED in Perry's throat and died unuttered. As if turned to wood by the glitter of those eyes, he stood rooted to the threshold, his hands white and wet on the sides of the doorframe. Then the glaring eyes narrowed; the drooling face beneath them wrinkled into a triumphant leer. A peal of low laughter came from Merritt's shadowed lips.

The voice that croaked from those lips was hardly more than a cracked whisper, barely audible, above the pounding of rain on the porch. "You see, Milton Perry, I have returned!"

He took a step forward; his sodden boots sucked on the wet boards. "Yes—I have returned to visit you." He stopped again and laughed mirthlessly. His shriveled body, wrapped in a monstrous black overcoat whose upturned collar all but concealed his features, was a thing risen from the grave—a black ghoul-shape that blended with the dark of night as if spawned by that very darkness.

A clawlike hand stabbed out. A bony forefinger pointed rigidly into Perry's bloodless face. "Listen to me, Milton Perry. In spite of the curse on you, you went ahead with your evil plans. Now it's too late! Too—late! Doom is on you. Sickness'll come, and madness. Before three days are past, you'll lie in an agony worse than death, away from all who love you.

"All alone you'll be, in a place of darkness and despair. And then death will come to shake hands with you, and I'll be waiting to lead you to the pits of torment." The cracked voice sank to a whisper. "You hear, Milton Perry. Before three days are past, you'll be like me, dead! You're cursed. The doom is on you. The breath of doom..."

Something let go in Perry's brain. A jangling scream tocsined from his lips and he lunged forward. This leering, mocking ghoul-shape before him was the cause of all his agony! This thing, this black monstrosity, that in life had been Benjamin Merritt, had brought doom to Fiskeville and death to the father of the girl Perry loved!

His lunging body surged over the threshold, arms outflung, hands clawing toward the death's-head that leered there in darkness.

But his hands failed to make contact. Rain had puddled the floor of the porch and made of it a sodden slippery surface that hurled him headlong. The ghoul shape moved sideways with a silent gliding rapidity that seemed no movement at all.

Perry reeled across the narrow veranda, flailing the dark with both arms as he sought to regain balance. Then his stumbling feet encountered emptiness; his contorted body hurtled into space, struck the veranda steps a glancing blow and crashed to the flagstoned path beyond.

Excruciating pain knifed one shoulder. A moan of agony filled Perry's throat and spilled into. the night. On the veranda above him, old Merritt chuckled in obscene triumph....

Perry rolled over once, twice, as a dog might roll after being struck by a speeding car. Then he lay still, with rain beating his limp body and a cold chill creeping through him from the wet stones beneath....

HE did not lose consciousness. Like a man condemned, he lay there in rain and darkness, waiting. This was the end. But why was that hideous shape so slow in descending the veranda steps to bend above him and put its vile hands on him? Surely the thing meant to destroy him!

He remembered, then, the words that had issued from those death-rotted lips. "Before three days are past...." So he had three days left to live. Three days of unbearable agony and loneliness. Death would be a thousand times more merciful if it came now! Three days of madness, of utter isolation... knowing that he could not seek help without bringing doom to those who tried to comfort him. God!

Three days. Benjamin Merritt had returned from the gloom of the grave to deliver the summons. Had come back with dark eyes glowing, corpse-face iridescent with gloating, to whisper those words of inescapable doom.

Perry groaned, clawed the flagstones in an effort to rise. Old Merritt's guttural words were still in his brain, mocking him, watering the blood that chilled his heart. Numb with a cold not of the rain that beat down on him, he had no courage left, no hope, no desire to fight. What good would come of fighting, now?

Then he heard footsteps, and at the foot of the flagstone walk the gate creaked open.

Groping hands pawed Perry's shoulders. A familiar voice, the voice of Everett Latham, said hoarsely: "Good Lord, Perry, what's happened?"

Perry stared into the face above him. Violently he wrenched his shoulders, tried to squirm clear of the man's friendly hands. "Leave me alone!" Strange, that that shrill, half-mad voice should be emanating from his own lips! "Leave me alone! Don't touch me!"

"Don't—touch you?"

"You'll die the way the others died! Don't come near me, in the name of God—"

"Nonsense, man!" Latham reached down, found a grip and hauled Perry erect. "You're ill. Come inside, out of the rain."

A scream convulsed Perry's face. "I warn you, Latham. Don't say I didn't warn you. The curse—"

"Oh, bother the curse! Only an idiot would believe in such things!"

Gently Latham put an arm around those sodden shoulders, aided Perry in climbing the porch steps. The sounds that spilled from Perry's throat were low sobs; the terror in his glazed eyes did not diminish.

This would mean another victim! Blackness clutched at his soul, racked him with torment. Weakly he fought to free himself from the strong hands that supported him, but Latham would not permit it.

Inside, Latham steered him to a chair and lowered him into it, stood back and gazed at him with an expression of deep pity. "I'd have come sooner, old man, but I had to wait at Jordon's house for Janice to return. Someone had to stay with her mother. What the devil have you been up to? What were you doing out there on the walk?"

Perry licked dry lips, shuddered. "*He* was here."

"He? Who?"

"Merritt. I'm not mad, Latham. Not—yet. Old Merritt came here to—to warn me."

Latham scowled, took a short step backward as if suddenly afraid. "You *are* ill. Let me get a doctor, Perry."

"No, no. My God, don't you realize—"

"But Merritt couldn't have come here." Latham's voice was soft, soothing, the voice of one who sought to calm a terrified child. "He died. Don't you remember, old man? Old Merritt is dead."

"I know. But he was here."

"Nonsense! You were seeing things, that's all. Your nerves are upset." Firm fingers touched Perry's shoulder and clung there reassuringly. "It's nothing but nerves. You've been through a lot, Perry. Just take things easy for a while. I'll make some coffee to straighten you out."

He was gone, into the kitchen. Perry sat motionless, conscious only of a numbing fear in his heart and the dull throbbing of rain against shut windows. Why had Latham come? Why had not a merciful God warned him to stay away? Now it was too late. The black tentacles of old Merritt's curse had reached out to enfold another innocent victim.

"Too late," Perry moaned. "It's too late...."

Vaguely he was aware of comforting, everyday sounds from the kitchen: the gurgle of running water, a hissing sound as Latham ignited a burner of the gas-range. But they were merely a background for the thoughts that crawled like bloated slugs through his racked brain.

Latham was trying to help him. That was funny, now. He and Latham had always been cold toward each other, because of their mutual love for Janice. Yet in time of trouble Latham had come, had forgotten that coldness. And Janice had stayed away.

Thank God she had! Otherwise she, too, would be doomed!

Footsteps scraped on the threshold and Perry forced his lolling head up, gazed dully as Latham came toward him.

"Here...." Latham bent above him, held forward a steaming cup that contained black coffee. "Here, drink this. You're just upset, old man. Coffee's good for the nerves."

Perry drank, mumbled his thanks.

"And don't worry about old Merritt's visit," Latham said softly, persuasively. "You were seeing things, that's all. You're on the verge of a nervous breakdown, and jangled nerves do queer things to us sometimes. You'll be all right."

"You don't understand," Perry muttered.

"I think I do. But don't worry about it, and don't worry about me, either." A grin wrinkled Latham's thin face. "A curse works only when you believe in it, Perry. Psychology, that's all. And it won't affect me because I just don't believe. Nothing's going to happen to me."

"It—doesn't work unless you believe in it?"

"That's the big secret. Now you just take care of yourself. Pack yourself off to bed and I'll see that Janice is here in the morning to look after you." Again Latham's hand found Perry's shoulder and exerted pressure. "She loves you, you know."

He straightened, stepped back. "I'll run along now. See you later. If the nerves get you again, give me a ring on the phone and I'll hustle over here. But you won't need me. You'll be all right. I'm sure of it."

He walked to the door, working his arms into the sleeves of a rubber raincoat. From the doorway he called a cheery, "Goodnight, Perry." Then the outer door opened, closed, and Perry was alone.

VERY slowly, Perry got out of his chair and dragged his weary body up the staircase to the bedroom on the floor above. Sobbing, he flung himself on the bed....

But sleep was a mockery, filled with a procession of garish nightmares that paraded one after another through his warped mind. Old Merritt's guttural voice intoned again from shrunken lips: "Sickness'll come, and madness. Before three days are past, you'll lie all alone in an agony worse than death. The breath of doom is on you...."

Ora Fiske was in the room, too, sitting as he had sat in the jail office, fatly important, somehow triumphant. And Walzek, smiling a smile so benign that its very benignity was replete with evil.

And Fiske's followers, leering and pointing and screaming words of fanatical triumph. "You would have desecrated Jason's Knoll, where the hand of God preserved our forefathers from doom. Now the doom is on *you*, for your sin! Three days...."

He awoke trembling in every muscle, sat up in bed with a convulsive jerk and stared into the room's darkness. And the room was empty again. Rain made a hollow dirge on the roof and the storm sang a funeral singsong. The chamber was black with that blackness which comes just before dawn.

Perry put damp hands to his quivering face, and the hands were cold as the fleshless bones of a corpse! The darkness mocked him; the voice of the storm was a muttering cry of evil that spiked his soul with dread. Frantically he pushed the bedclothes away and lurched erect.

He knew then that the threat of old Merritt had taken effect. "Sickness'll come, and madness...." He was sick! And before long madness would rush upon him out of darkness....

A numbness was in his head and his trembling body was cold as ice. When he removed his hand from the bedpost and ventured a step forward, the room swam before him, the floor billowed, the ceiling formed a distorted angle that leaned into limitless space. His feet followed a zigzag course to the door and carried him in staggering flight to the head of the staircase. On the stairs he would have pitched headlong had not his hands clutched the banister.

"Sickness'll come, and madness...."

What time was it? How many centuries had passed since Latham had bent above him, offering words of comfort? He stumbled along the downstairs hall and peered at the clock, but the clock-face was a blur before his eyes—a human face grinning derisively. Sobbing, he found a light-switch, stared again and saw that the hour was four-thirty. Four-thirty a.m.

He could not stay longer in this house of torment. Every fiber within him shrieked at him to get out, get away. He looked down at himself out of bloodshot eyes and saw that he was dressed. Dressed in the same dark clothes he had worn the day before, but they were crumpled now and flecked with lint from the bed-sheets.

He groped toward the door, stopped again and gazed dully at the telephone. If only he could talk to Janice, even for just a moment! Talk to her and hear the soft murmur of her voice, pour out the anguish in his heart! She would listen surely. She did not hate him that much!

His hand clawed the phone, then with a convulsive jerk came away. No, no, he could not call her! Old Merritt's curse—there was no knowing how horribly far that monstrous threat could reach, how hellishly long were its sucking tentacles of doom. If those tentacles coiled around the girl he loved, it would be the end of life, of hope, of everything!

"Oh my God," he moaned, "if only I could talk to someone! I'm so lonely!"

What had Latham said? "If you need me...." He could go to Latham's house, leave this abode of madness behind. Latham lived on the far side of town, in a small brown cottage with an older sister and a mother who for years had been confined to a wheel-chair. Latham would talk to him, comfort him.

RAIN lashed his bare head as he walked. Rain drenched him and soaked the clothes that clung to his shivering body. But the chill of wet darkness was as nothing compared with the chill within him that numbed his muscles. Cool air drove some of the sickness out of him, but not all. He staggered, peered ahead with wide eyes that strained to see through an unnatural mist, a mist that came from his brain and was thicker, denser than the darkness.

He walked in a daze, hardly knowing the route he followed. Mud sucked at his feet; a biting wind whined in his face and drove slanting sheets of water against his hunched shoulders. In a little while it would be daylight. That thought comforted him. Then another thought came, and brought wild hope to his throbbing heart.

Latham! Latham would be the final test of the power behind old Merritt's curse! If he were alive, if he were well, it would be proof that the curse was but a black mummery created by Walzek, Fiske, or some of the others!

Latham's house loomed ahead through the downpour, and Perry quickened his stumbling pace, clawed the gate open and labored up the veranda's wooden steps.

No lights glowed in the structure before him. No sound penetrated the hollow drumming of the rain. For an instant he hesitated, felt as if he were doing an evil thing by arousing sleeping people at this hour. Then his quivering hand found the bell.

He heard the drone of the bell inside, heard it die to silence. Half a mile distant in the town square, the clock on the courthouse tower boomed five times. Five o'clock. It would be daylight now, but for the rain. The darkness was a grey murk that crowded around him.

Again he thumbed the bell and waited. The courthouse clock had stopped striking. A light glowed behind the frosted door-panel and footsteps were audible beyond the barrier. Perry held his breath, stood trembling. A shadow blurred the light. The knob turned slowly.

Then the door opened—and Perry took a faltering step backward away from the threshold. Eyes wide, he stared in horror at the human thing that stood there. Rain lashed against him and he was unaware of its savage impact.

That human thing was Everett Latham. Leprous-white hands gripped the sides of the doorframe. Last night's smile was not on Latham's lips; his eyes no longer were filled with sympathetic understanding.

The man's face was a gaunt grey gargoyle empty of life. His lips were curled in a snarl, displaying blackened teeth. His cheeks were thin layers of flesh sucked in around bulging muscles. Illness—some horrible, devouring illness had claimed him!

Words came hollowly from the man's shapeless mouth. Glaring with dark orbs he said sluggishly: "What—do you want?"

But Perry had no reply. Blood had ebbed from his own face. His own eyes were protruding so far from their sockets that pain stabbed through them. What had he thought a little while ago? This would be the final test of old Merritt's curse? God!

"Leave me alone," Latham said hollowly. "Go away and leave me alone. Haven't you done enough to me already?"

Perry did not move, could not. That agony-racked face fascinated him and he stared into it, seeing every horrible detail, every pit of shadow. And the pain-glazed eyes returned his stare without blinking.

Then suddenly the gargoyle face convulsed. Blind rage filled it, as Latham's crooked hands lashed up and stabbed forward. "Get out! Get out and don't ever come back! You're a demon out of hell, Milton Perry! The curse is on you...."

Perry stumbled backward, turned with a shriek and clawed his way down the steps. The gate clanged shut behind him and he ran—ran blindly through fog and rain and darkness, without knowing where his feet took him.

Long minutes later, when he stumbled up the steps of his own empty house, night had crept away before a sunless dawn. The darkness in his own soul was far greater than the darkness around him.

CHAPTER FOUR

ALONE WITH DOOM

"*ALL ALONE* you'll be, in a place of darkness and despair, away from all who love you. Sickness'll come, and madness... and then death will come to shake hands...."

Old Merritt had said that. Old Merritt had crept from the grave to come in the darkness and mutter that grim threat. And now, standing in ankle-deep mud on the sidewalk, Perry stared back at the porch where the corpse-creature had stood while delivering the ultimatum.

He shuddered, and glanced down at the bulging suitcase in his hand. By leaving Fiskeville and going away alone, he was doing exactly what Merritt had prophesied. But what else could he do? An aura of death clung to him; hideous destruction lay in the touch of his hands, in the stare of his bloodshot eyes. *"Death and doom to everyone you love...."*

A sob shook his aching body as he turned away. This was the end. This was goodbye to friends and loved ones, to the sleepy New England town that claimed his affection. This was farewell to Janice and to hope.

The hour was still early, the town still slumbering in a winding-sheet of grey fog. Shades were drawn in the houses on both sides of the narrow street; the houses themselves were distorted shapes looming through drizzle, staring in grim silence as Perry trudged along the sidewalk.

He had left his car, last night, in front of the Jordon home. Unless someone had moved it....

No one had. In the house beyond that familiar white fence, a light was burning. He stood by the car's dripping fender and stared, and his eyes were wet with more than rain-mist.

If he climbed those steps and touched the small white button in the door-frame, someone would answer. Janice would answer. She would open the door and, for the last time, he would be able to look into her face.

The thought spawned resolution and he took a sudden step forward. But resolution died when his hand fell on the gate-latch. Still staring, he backed away, shut his eyes to the temptation of that lighted window. A groan died in his throat. He heard again old Merritt's croaking voice: *"Death and doom to everyone you love."*

This time old Merritt would be wrong! Wrong! A snarl gurgled against Perry's twisted lips. He turned away, forced himself to walk to the car. And as the car's damp engine coughed to life and the machine sputtered slowly away from that lighted window, he did not look back.

Fiskeville faded behind him in a sea of mist. Ahead lay lonely country roads leading into desolation. And the clicking of the windshield wiper made words.

"The breath of doom be on you, Milton Perry! Before three days...."

He knew his destination. Twenty-odd miles from Fiskeville a narrow dirt road wound through deep woods and circled the base of Baldtop Mountain, and a snake-track trail, beginning there, wormed up the mountainside. Up there, on the shore of a small pond that had no name, stood a weather-beaten, dilapidated hunting-lodge—his own lodge, built years ago and seldom used except for occasional week-end hunting trips.

With food and other necessities he could hide there forever from prying eyes. None would suspect his whereabouts. Even Janice would not guess.

Alone, all alone in a forgotten wilderness hideout, he could fight his own battle with sickness and death. And with madness.

He drove slowly, and no cars came toward him. Rain throbbed its dirge on the roof; water cascaded into dense underbrush on both sides as the machine's wheels lurched into hidden pitfalls in the unpaved road. The wiper counted minutes into eternities and mocked him with its endless beat that was so like the laborious pounding of his own heart.

Once, glancing into the mirror, he saw that his face was haggard with sickness, his eyes red-rimmed from staring. But it did not matter. Even the despair and dull loneliness that gripped him did not matter now.

Miles from the village, he turned the car up a rutted road, drove it on and on through a quagmire of red mud. At last he stopped it. Sliding wearily from the seat, Perry stood clutching the car door.

The sickness had wormed into his legs. Minutes passed before he was able to rope his supplies together, and lock the car, and trudge into the sodden trail that led ever upward through deep woods.

That climb was torment, the trail a patch through Hades. Hours later when he came in sight of the ramshackle lodge building, breath husked in his throat and his heart hammered wildly in his chest. He staggered the last few strides.

His fingers were ice-cold as they fumbled with the rusty padlock on the lodge door.

He slumped then into an old rustic chair before the fireplace, and was but dimly aware of the whining storm-wind that sought ingress through walls of huge pine-logs. This was desolation. Here he could be alone, all one, with no fear of bringing doom to other innocent victims.

And he was tired, ill. His head lolled. The wail of the wind became a muffled, half-audible human voice, intoning words: "*Three days… Then death will come to shake hands.…*"

He slept.

THE rising fury of the storm awoke him and he sat suddenly stiff, his hands clawing the rough chair-arms. Seconds passed while he stared about him in bewilderment. Then he remembered, and laughed hoarsely. Rising, he threw pine-chips and logs into the fireplace and built a fire.

What time was it? He had no watch, and the battered alarm-clock on the fireplace mantel had stopped months ago. Stumbling to a window, he drew aside the dusty curtains and peered out.

But the storm had brought artificial darkness, blurring the huge trees whose tops bent under the wind's savage onslaught. No man could judge time by the noisesome murk that held the lodge in its maw.

Yet he must have slept a long while. Hunger gnawed at him, and the sickness within him had increased alarmingly. The floor swayed beneath him as he turned, made his way slowly toward the kitchen. His outthrust hands clawed at tables and chairs in an effort to keep him erect.

Three rooms the lodge possessed—kitchen and bedroom and living-room. In the kitchen an ancient wood-stove loomed like a pot-bellied old man, and pots and pans hung in rusty array along the wall.

He made a fire, drank hot black coffee and stuffed food into his mouth. But the food made him ill and quickened the vicious throbbing of his heart. An hour passed while he slumped over the kitchen table, his head in his hands. Then he returned to the living-room. He knew then that he had been in the lodge a long while, for the room was gloomy with the darkness of night.

When he poured oil into a greasy lamp and put a match to the wick, the reluctant flame cast crawling shadows over walls and floor and ceiling. Despair and loneliness stalked the storm-racked enclosure, taunting him with storm-born voices of derision.

Three days. Then death....

Perry stood wide-legged, stared with bloodshot eyes and felt self-control ebbing out of him. Someone in the room was shrieking wildly, in a voice that tocsined above the muffled roar of wind and rain: "I can't stand it! My God, I'll go mad!"

The voice was his own.

That night he made himself think of Ora Fiske and Anthony Walzek and Sheriff Gates and all the others who had reason to hate him. Was it not possible that Hallam Jordon had been murdered—poisoned, perhaps, through the food served to him in his jail cell? Gates would have served that food. Perhaps Ora Fiske had helped prepare it....

Yet, even if that were true, it would not account for the death and resurrection of old Merritt, and for the hideous disease which had attacked Everett Latham. It would not explain those withered flowers and other dark happenings.

He wondered again what time it was. Probably around midnight. He was ill, and when he stood up to peer into a mirror he saw a bloodless, hollow-cheeked face that startled him.

Merritt had given him three days. It would not take that long....

He fell asleep in the chair before the fireplace. Asleep, he did not know that the storm increased steadily in violence throughout the night hours; nor did he see the first grey murk of dawn. Nor did he hear the first muffled knockings which in time, through their very persistence, aroused him.

When he did awake, he gripped the chair-arms with thin bony fingers and jerked his head around, and stared. Stared at the door. And scowled, in bewilderment.

Someone was out there. But who? Who of the townspeople could know that he had come here to this forgotten hideaway? Few of Fiskeville's residents even knew of this place. Latham knew, and Janice, and perhaps Sheriff Gates. But....

Again that insistent thumping boomed hollowly through the muffled shriek of storm-wind and the endless drumming of rain against shut windows. He pushed himself slowly erect, tiptoed furtively to a window. One thing he knew—whoever saw him now would be shocked by his appearance. If they had come expecting to see the Milton Perry of a few days ago, the ambitious young manufacturer who had striven so hard to put Fiskeville on the map, they would cringe from him as from a graveyard ghoul! Well, he had not invited them!

His face close to the rain-splashed glass, he peered out, tried to see who stood there at the door. But it was dark out there. Someone was there, but he could see only a shadowed shape.

Then suddenly he stiffened, straight-armed himself away from the window and stood with bated breath. Out there a voice was calling his name. "Milt! Milton Perry! *Please* let me in!"

He would know that voice anywhere. It was *her* voice!

HE stood staring at the door, and terror crept like a living thing into his wasted face. Of all people, *she* must not get in! The others he no longer cared about. If they were mad enough to seek him, knowing the horrible doom that exuded from the very pores of his emaciated body, that was their own concern. But not Janice! Merciful God, if she came over that threshold of death she would try to help him, as Latham had tried. And then....

He saw Latham's face, a mask of disease-eaten ugliness, glaring at him with dull accusation.... Then, eyes wide and bloodshot, Perry was standing flat against the locked door, his nails clawing the rough pine panels as he shouted hysterically: "You can't come in! I won't let you in here! Go back where you came from!"

The answer came above the howl of the storm. "Milt! Milt Perry! Are you in there?" Evidently she had not heard him. The storm had become a vicious screaming monster during the hours of darkness, and through its mad din she had not heard his voice....

"You can't come in!" he shrieked again. "Do you hear? I won't let you!"

She was rattling the latch now, and thumping at the door with a clenched fist. She must know he was somewhere inside. Probably she had seen his car parked at the foot of the Baldtop Mountain trail, miles below, where he always left it when coming here. She had been here two or three times last summer, and would know that if the place were empty now the padlock would be on the outside.

But she had not heard his voice. Why was that? He bellowed again with his lips close to the heavy barrier, and knew the answer. What he had thought to be a hoarse shout was only a husky whisper. He had no voice, no strength.

She had stopped knocking, was no longer calling his name. Breath sighed from his wasted lips and he stood stock-still, listening. Then suddenly he whirled. She had gone to a window! Her small fist was thudding against the glass. Her face, strangely white and unreal, was pressed against the pane, peering in.

She saw him. Her lips moved, and shrill words ate into the room. "Milt! Let me in! I won't harm you. I only want to help you!"

He stood rooted to the floor, shaking his head foolishly from side to side, mumbling words that she could not possibly hear. "No. You can't. You mustn't. Don't you know what will happen if you come near me? Don't you know what happened to you father and to Latham and—and to the flowers?"

She was gone. Gone so abruptly that for a moment the imprint of her features seemed to linger on the wet glass. He stared, stumbled forward with both arms outflung, bony hands clawing space. "Oh God, I want you, Jan! I need you!" Then he laughed hoarsely, and tears filled his red-rimmed eyes.

She had seen the hideous transformation in him, and the shock of looking into his changed face had frightened her away. She would not come back now. That was a good thing. If she did get over her fright and come back later, it would be too late. Old Merritt had said three days, but he knew better....

Then suddenly her face was again at the window. She peered in, stared straight at him. Her fist gripped a jagged stone that slapped the pane. Glass broke. She struck again and again, and more glass broke; wind-driven rain shrieked into the room, drenching the floor. The girl's bare arms, wet and gleaming, were on the sill; her head and shoulders loomed through the aperture.

Perry stared in gurgling horror. His eyes bulged, and he gaped at the mop of drenched hair that hung over her face. That face was white, too white. Something had drained the blood from it. Something horrible....

He lurched backward, away from it. He could not stop her now! If he laid hands on her or even went close to her, he would bring doom on the person he loved most in all the world. And if he let her clamber in through the window, she would stare at him for a moment in horror, and then, because she loved him, she would rush forward and try to help him!

"Go back!" he screamed at her. "You don't know what you're doing! Go back!"

But she came on, oblivious to his words.

PERRY whirled, lunged toward the kitchen doorway. In there he had dumped the supplies he had lugged from town. Madness seared his heart and told him a way out.

He heard the girl's feet thud to the floor behind him as he ran. But he was over the kitchen threshold then, and his flailing hand caught the door, flung it shut. The girl was shrilling his name hysterically, but the closing door muffled the tocsin of his voice.

The door had no lock. Frantically he flung a chair against it, wedged the chairtop beneath the protruding latch. That would hold her! He would have time enough....

His supplies lay in a corner, dumped there in a heap. On hands and knees he flopped beside them, fought sudden sickness while he pawed through canned goods, clothing. Cold sweat trickled down his forehead and stung his eyes, as salt might sting a raw wound. His groping fingers found a small brown bottle whose scarlet label read: POISON.

He had taken the bottle from the medicine cabinet at home, and had thought then: "If madness does come, even old Merritt cannot make me endure it!" Now the bottle would save him from more than madness. It would save him the horror of bringing doom to the girl who was out there in the other room, thumping wildly at the door!

He swayed erect, and hoarse laughter gurgled in his throat. Jan was putting her shoulder to the door now. The chair was groaning a protest against her determined onslaught. Her voice came in a sob through the creaking barrier. "Oh God, Milt, let me talk to you! I won't harm you...."

That—was funny. He stared at the door and laughed softly. What did she think? That he was afraid of her? That he didn't want her?

Want her! God, if she only knew how much he did want her! If she only knew how much he would give just to take her in his arms for one short minute before—

He looked down at the brown bottle and shuddered. His thin fingers clawed at the cork, but it was wedged deep in the brown-glass neck and would not loosen. Across the room, the door was groaning open!

He stepped suddenly backward, gripped the bottle in trembling fingers and slapped its thick neck against the iron edge of the stove. Glass broke and gashed his hand. His lips sucked a deep breath that shook his emaciated frame from head to foot.

Then, as the door burst inward and the girl stumbled toward him, he upended the jagged neck of the bottle in his mouth, tipped his head back, and drank.

Janice Jordon stopped with a jerk, stood swaying on spread legs and stared. The scarlet word POISON hung on a direct line with her wide eyes. She screamed.

The scream came from the depths of her soul and shrilled like a living thing through the storm-racked kitchen; but Perry did not hear. Agony came and went in his bloodless face. He lurched backward; the wall stopped him.

Leaning there like a propped-up corpse, he returned the girl's stare—and smiled. A look of contentment dislodged the pain in his eyes. The brown bottle dropped from his limp fingers.

With a bubbling sigh he slid to the floor and pitched forward, arms outflung....

CHAPTER FIVE
The Corpse Returns

PERRY DID not see Janice Jordon stumble forward and sink to her knees beside him. He did not see tears form in her eyes and splash on his gaping mouth as she turned him over and bent above him, sobbing out the torment in her heart.

Hysteria claimed her for a moment. Her slender hands clawed his shirt open; she pressed her damp cheek against his chest, listening for a heartbeat. Then a grim calmness came over her—the same strong fortitude which had steeled her forefathers when they had fought seemingly insurmountable odds on Jason's Knoll. She bowed her head above him, and a prayer whispered from her pale lips.

"Please God, let him live. I love him so...."

And then the blood of hardy pioneer ancestors ran red in her trembling body. For hours she worked over him, not frantically, not desperately, but with a deliberate stolidity that brought results.

When he opened his eyes at last and stared up at her through the mist that fogged his brain, a sob welled from her lips and she whispered almost inaudibly: "Thank God!"

Perry scowled, could not remember. Dully he peered into the face above him, turned his head and gazed at his blurred surroundings. He saw pine logs smouldering in a fireplace, saw a broken window where blankets and a faded quilt had been stuffed to keep out rain. Then, vaguely, he was conscious of familiar sounds—the clamoring howl of wind and the ceaseless thunder of rain beating at walls and roof.

She had carried him from the kitchen to the living-room and

somehow managed to lift his dead weight onto a couch. She had dragged that couch nearer the fire, and kept the fire going, and—brought him back to life.

The rest was but a haze of furtive memories, somehow black with evil. There had been a bottle. The cork would not come out, and he had broken the bottle against the stove....

He put a trembling hand on the girl's arm. Somehow he was not as sick as he had been. He was weak, pitifully weak, but that devouring ache had gone out of his body. That gnawing pain, as of demon hands inside him clawing viciously to reach his heart—it was gone now.

He tried to make words, but the words that choked in his throat were incoherent, foolish. "Oh my dear," he mumbled, over and over. "Oh—my dear...."

"You're not to talk," she told him firmly, and frowned down at him. But a smile of immeasurable happiness worked its way through the frown, and her eyes were glowing. "You're to lie still and get your strength back. The very idea, thinking you can take poison one minute and be up and about again the next instant!"

"The next—instant?"

"Well, it's been a bit longer than that, but you're still not yourself. Close your eyes now and try to sleep."

She closed his eyes for him, but he opened them again and looked steadily into her hovering face. He had been right about that face. It was not normal, not glowing with warm health as it should be. Something had sapped the color from her cheeks and put a dull glazed look in her eyes.

"You're not well," he whispered.

She was silent for a moment. Then: "You mustn't worry about me."

"But you're not well!"

"It's nothing. Nothing at all." She turned her face from his unblinking gaze. "I'm just tired."

Black dread wormed into his heart. Her denials meant nothing; loving him, she would not confess the truth. But he knew. She had been white and pale when she had peered in through the window, hours ago. *That* paleness might have been brought about by her effort of fighting through the storm. This gaunt hollowness of her cheeks, this dead glare that hung now in her eyes, was something else!

Old Merritt's curse....

He pushed himself up on rigid arms. "You can't stay here, Jan! You *can't!* Oh God, don't you see what's happening to you?"

"Nothing is happening," she said firmly, and pushed him down again. "I'm just tired. In a little while I'll be perfectly all right."

"No, no—"

"Will you be *still?*"

"Oh, my dear—"

She smoothed his hair back, and the touch of her fingers made him shudder. Her hand was cold and damp against his forehead. But she did not know; she did not realize....

A crafty gleam came into his eyes. He sighed, made an effort to seem relaxed. Quietly he said: "Listen, Jan. You could go back to town and bring a doctor. I'll give you the keys to my car. I'm not afraid to be left alone, dear."

She nodded. "I might do that later."

"Do it now. Take the keys and—"

"If you'll go to sleep, I'll consider it."

"Yes, yes—I'll go to sleep! I'll do anything you say...."

He closed his eyes, breathed deeply and evenly. God, if only she would heed his suggestion and leave him! It would take her a long while to fight through the storm and reach the car, then drive to Fiskeville and return. But in that time he could be gone—gone away, anywhere, where she would not find him!

And it might not be too late! The doctor would see that something was wrong with her, and would take care of her. Perhaps, under a doctor's care, she could fight old Merritt's curse....

He feigned sleep, released his grip on her ice-cold arm and let his hand slide limply to the couch. With his eyes shut he sensed, rather than knew, that she bent closer to peer into his face. Her breath was cold on his cheek. Then, a moment later, he knew that she had risen from the couch, and he lay utterly without motion, listening to the slow click of her heels as she paced cautiously across the room.

She was going—leaving him. Elation surged within him and he had to suppress the cry of joy that welled against his lips. She would get away in time....

Warily he opened his eyes, peered beneath drooping lids. Then he frowned. The girl had not gone to the door, but had paced stealthily toward a window and was standing motionless, one hand on the faded curtain, as she stared out through the rain-washed glass.

Fear was on her face!

PERRY lay tense, the fingers of both hands clenched in the couch cover beneath him. Something Jan saw out there had frightened her. What could it be, in the height of such a storm? Had someone followed her to the lodge?

The answer came with nerve-racking abruptness. Above the wail of storm wind and beating rain, the door quivered to a sudden heavy thud, as of a clenched fist hammering sluggishly for admission. Janice Jordon pressed closer to the window, stared out, and took a sudden step backward. Her lips opened; the cry that jangled from her throat was a scream of stark terror, a vibrant note of fear that wailed wildly through the room.

But the scream was of short duration. With sudden courage the girl hurled herself at the door, both hands outflung to seize the heavy iron bolt. That bolt was out of its socket. Evidently, while Perry had lain unconscious, the girl had opened the door and gone outside. Probably she had gone out to repair the broken window....

She was too late now. Before her groping hands could reach the bolt and slam it home, the door jarred open, clattered violently against the wall. Eyes wide with horror, Janice fell back, screamed again as her gaze encountered the drenched, dripping shape that filled the aperture.

Driving rain came with the intruder as he stepped forward. The storm howled about him, beat at him in mad fury. But Milton Perry had no thought for the storm. Staring with enormous eyes at that hunched, drooling shape, he heaved himself off the bed, lurched erect on unsteady legs and flattened in horror against the wall.

Slowly the intruder advanced, reached out with fearful lack of haste and forced the door shut behind him. Leprous white fingers closed the bolt, snapped the dangling padlock and withdrew the key. Turning, the invader raised his head to peer with sunken eyes at the terrified girl. And then, with equal deliberateness, he swayed his bloated body and leveled his gaze at Perry.

That face, drooling water from its hideous cheeks, was a ghastly grey horror, a corpse-face risen in unholy triumph from the black depths of the grave. That bloated, rain-soaked body was the same living-dead shape which had stood in darkness on the veranda of Milton Perry's cottage, cursing him.

The intruder was Benjamin Merritt!

The terror-shriek that welled to Perry's lips died unuttered. His back to the wall, he stood wide-legged, the splayed fingers of his outstretched hands clawing the wall-timbers. Less than twenty paces from him, across the room, Janice Jordon seemed incapable of movement, seemed unable to cry out.

A snarl curled the intruder's foul lips; his evil gaze swept the girl's rigid figure. "So—you came to share your lover's fate, my dear. You came to be with him in his hour of agony." Low laughter croaked from his throat. "I expected as much. I am not surprised."

He advanced a step, stopped again. The room's darkness, spawned by the storm without, seemed to swirl about him like a living winding-sheet as he glared across the chamber into Perry's bloodless face. Water dripped from the down-turned brim of his sodden hat and the falling drops beat time to his guttural words.

"Were you foolish enough to think you might escape the curse of Benjamin Merritt? Never, Milton Perry. Benjamin Merritt himself has come to make sure the curse does not fail!"

Shadows masked the leer that creased those uncouth features. Sodden shoes scraped the floor; Merritt's hunched body sidled forward. Slowly, relentlessly, his arms snaked out and those leprous white hands, curled like albino spiders, reached menacingly toward Perry's throat.

For an instant terror held Perry rigid. Then out of that same terror was born a desperation that gave him strength to lunge sideways. He had no eyes for Janice, yet knew that she stood stricken with fear, her slender bosom heaving with the ebb and flow of her breath, her eyes bulging, her face drained of all color.

Clawing the wall, Perry strove frantically to escape the ghoul's attack. Escape? How could one escape a creature from the dead, a monster who was alive and yet had no claim to life? How could one gaze into that rotted death-mask and even *hope* to escape? Yet for the girl's sake he had to fight, had to find some way....

He moved, but the oncoming fiend moved with him, continuing that hellish advance. Twin spider-hands reached out.

Perry sucked breath, leaped wildly for the kitchen doorway. If he could make it, hurl himself into the other room, he might find some weapon with which to defend himself. If that cadaverous shape lived, it could be robbed of life, beaten to bloody pulp!

His fingers raked the door-frame, but he was too late. Other fingers, cold and wet, fastened from behind in the flesh of his throat. He screamed, and the scream came from the innermost depths of a soul racked with terror. Then, blindly, he was fighting.

He fought, but had no strength. His clenched fists beat against the leering corpse-face that hung above him; his nails raked rotten flesh, clawed at the demon's eyes and mouth—but took no toll. Inexorably those leprous fingers tightened in his throat, strangling him, and the hungry, fearful face hung within inches of his agonized eyes. He gasped for breath, caught none. His efforts grew weaker.

Then, from nowhere, a hurtling shape fell upon the monster's hunched back; slender hands sought to claw those murderous fingers from Perry's neck. His bulging eyes, glazed with pain, saw the determined face of Janice Jordon; as if from a great distance he heard the shrill words that jangled from the girl's lips.

"You let him go! Let him go or I'll kill you! Oh God—"

Old Merritt's crushing fingers released their grip, flung Perry aside. With a violent snarl the fiend whirled on braced legs, caught the girl in his embrace and slapped a wet white palm against her face. So savage was the blow that the sound of it was like the slap of a wet towel against tortured flesh. Janice stumbled backward, cried out in agony.

That scream was Perry's undoing. Blind with rage, he stumbled forward. And a clenched fist leaped to meet him, blasted his face and hurled him back against the couch.

Weakly he struggled to rise, and could not. Darkness, choked with the shrieking voice of the girl he loved and the low, guttural laughter of the hell-spawned ghoul before him, sucked him into a black maw where silence reigned supreme....

HE thought at first that death had claimed him, that the curse of old Benjamin Merritt had at last brought an end to the torturous ordeal of living. His eyelids seemed weighted, would not open. His body was numb with a numbness that must surely be part of eternal rest.

Then, somehow, his eyes twitched open and he was staring—staring at a strange figure that stood erect before the black maw of the fireplace. Bewilderment fogged his brain and he tried to lean forward, to peer through the grey mist that hung before his face. But his body would not move.

That figure, too, was surely a part of death. It could be nothing else. Yet it stood in familiar surroundings. The fireplace, the heavy pine-log walls, the bare, dusty living-room of the lodge....

But why should a near-naked woman be standing there, staring at him with eyes so very wide, so very full of fear? Who was she?

Realization came slowly as he gazed at the girl's pale flesh, stared in bewilderment at the firm whiteness of her half uncovered breasts, the gentle curves of her thighs and legs. Bits of white silk were all that adorned that lovely body. How could a girl be so lovely, so very lovely, and yet be so terrified about something?

Abruptly, then, full consciousness returned, and horror stabbed his soul. "Jan!" The word choked in his throat as he tried to lunge forward.

Cruel ropes dug into his arms and ankles, holding him back. With wide eyes he stared down at himself, saw that he was roped in a straight-backed chair whose rigid legs were forked through the iron cross-bar of the couch.

He was a prisoner! But where was the corpse-faced horrible who had overpowered him? Mutely he stared around the room. It was empty except for himself and for the girl who stood nearly naked against the fireplace.

She, too, was a captive. Rusty chains encircled her bare ankles and were locked around an iron bar that extended the length of the fireplace. Other chains secured her slender wrists....

He recognized those chains. They had been unhooked from some of the many steel traps that lay in a cupboard in the kitchen. But where was the fiend who had discovered them there and made such unholy use of them? What—what did the monster intend to do to Jan?

Words gurgled in Perry's throat and he strained forward, whispered the girl's name. "Jan! Jan! What has he done to you? Oh God, if he's harmed you—"

The girl, too, found a voice, after staring at him for a soul-racking eternity. "He hasn't harmed me, Milt. Not—yet. But I can't get loose. I've tried so hard—"

"Where is he?"

"He—he went—"

The answer came from another source. A sound of scuffing footsteps rasped above the moan of the storm, and Janice was suddenly rigid, gazing past Perry's bound body toward the kitchen doorway. With an effort, Perry jerked his head around. Through that doorway came the hunched, menacing shape of old Merritt.

Hate blazed in Merritt's deep-sunk eyes as he planted himself before Perry's trussed body. The sodden brim of his hat still shaded his gaunt face, but Perry, staring upward in wide-eyed horror, saw those thin lips move, heard the guttural words that rumbled from them.

"I have made a fire in the stove. Soon it will be hot enough. Do you understand what I mean, Milton Perry? Soon it will be hot enough...."

Foul laughter chuckled deep in his throat. The monster leaned closer; bloodless fingers tore Perry's shirt, ripped the undershirt beneath and bared the flesh of his heaving chest. Across the room Janice Jordon caught a sudden sharp breath of horror, anticipating what was to come.

"You think I am returned from the grave?" Merritt leered. "No, I am not that kind of creature. Illness did this hideous thing to my face and body, Milton Perry. Illness that resulted from the shock that seized me in the courthouse, when you aroused my righteous fury. But I did not die. They thought they buried me, but they buried an empty box!"

He laughed, and the laugh was a succession of throaty croaks, barely audible above the voice of the storm. "Tonight is mine, Milton Perry. For years I have loved a beautiful creature who would have none of me. Now she stands there, naked—" A bony forefinger stabbed toward the fireplace—"and in a little while she will come to me willingly, and be grateful for the chance. When the fire is hot enough...."

He paced slowly backward to the kitchen doorway, his glittering eyes maintaining their unholy glare of triumph, eagerly devouring the expression of terror that stiffened Perry's face. Then he was gone.

With strength that he did not know he possessed, Perry strained at the ropes that held him. The effort was futile. Perspiration stained his forehead, ran from his face and dripped on his bare chest. Across the room Janice Jordon gazed at him with imploring eyes, and her lips worked soundlessly as if praying to a merciful God to give him strength.

Then footsteps were again audible. Old Merritt reappeared in the doorway. This time, one of those leprous hands was outthrust, gripping a pair of long-handled pliers. And in the biting jaws lay a three-inch steel nail that glowed with pulsing redness in the semi-dark of the room!

Incapable of movement, Perry focused his unwavering gaze on that glowing spike and felt the blood in his veins turn to water. He knew now the significance of those guttural words: "Soon the fire will be hot enough...."

Slowly the monster advanced. And that scarlet shaft, pulsing like a naked, bloody heart, moved toward Milton Perry's bared chest!

CHAPTER SIX

BRANDED BY DEATH

TERROR PUT strength in Perry's emaciated body. Incoherent words shrilled from his lips, not pleading for mercy but wildly threatening old Merritt with death and destruction. Madly he strained at his bonds, writhed with such force that the chair groaned in protest under him.

But the bonds held. The long-handled pliers, with that red-hot nail gripped in their jaws, came nearer... nearer.... The nail made contact.

Tortured flesh writhed as the glowing steel pressed home. Madness leaped in Perry's eyes, blazed in his brain. In agony unbearable, he clenched his teeth to hold back the shriek that welled against them. An acrid odor of burning flesh choked his nostrils. The blood in his rigid body ran hot, carrying pain to the farthest nerve-ends.

Then the sizzling sound ceased; the glowing nail retreated, leaving a charred, smoking wound in tortured flesh. Old Merritt's lips curled in a sadistic leer of anticipation.

"Is it so very hard to bear, my friend? But wait! This is only a sample. Next time my little red finger of torment caresses the throat. And then, unless this beautiful creature requests me to be merciful—" He turned his head, grinned fiendishly at the sobbing girl who stood by the fireplace— "unless she is kind to you and begs me to desist, *I burn your eyes out!*"

Like a great ape, Merritt waddled forward, glared into the girl's stricken face. "You see my dear, I have desired you for a very long time. I even entertained hopes of making you my wife. But you refused me and gave your love to another." His leering lips curled on a snarl; one of his leprous hands glided forward to touch pale flesh that shrank from his caress.

"This night is mine, my dear. I planned it very carefully. No, it was not alone for you that I planned it. I had other motives which I may confess later, when you are nestled in my arms. But—" and the words rumbled nasally from lips that barely parted to release them— "this night shall be the consummation of all my desires. This night I shall destroy your unworthy lover and take you in my arms, and in one night I shall crowd all the satisfaction and delight that I had hoped to spread over long years. Now—will you come to me willingly?"

Janice Jordon had courage. Loathing, not terror, filled her smouldering eyes. Fists clenched, she crouched like an enraged cat against the fireplace. "You—you beast!"

"But you will soon change your mind, my dear. Wait and see!"

With a shrug, Merritt turned, paced slowly past Perry's bound body and vanished into the kitchen. Again, significant sounds found their way into the torture-room, to curdle the blood in Perry's veins and drain color from Janice Jordon's face. The girl stared at Perry, cried out in a broken whisper, "Oh God, what shall I do? He'll kill you unless—unless I promise—"

"If he lays a hand on you," Perry snarled, "I'll tear his rotten heart out!"

Then, from the very absurdity of his vow, he wanted suddenly to laugh, to go mad....

In the doorway, old Merritt stood watching, then scuffed slowly forward. Once again those long-handled pliers gripped a glowing shaft of metal. Perry's eyes widened, stared at the implement of torture until his bulging eyeballs themselves were streaked with scarlet.

"No, no!" he sobbed. "Don't—"

"It is not for you to say, my unhappy friend." A low chuckle accompanied Merritt's vibrant words. "It is for her. Perhaps she is willing to see you writhe in torment. Perhaps even the smell of burning flesh will not move her. Yet she loves you, and I think that when she sees those dark eyes of yours transformed to sightless black pits of burned flesh...."

No sound came from Perry's tight lips as the glowing nail made contact. His body stiffened with a convulsive jerk; the cords in his neck stood out like livid whip-welts. But he did not scream.

Slowly, relentlessly, the heated torture tool left a trail of agony across the quivering flesh of his neck. Then, rising slowly, it hung suspended before his eyes, so close that the heat seared his throbbing eyeballs and singed the dark lashes above them.

If those leprous hands moved a quarter-inch nearer....

EVERY nerve in Perry's body shrieked a mad cacophony of terror, yet no sound left his quivering lips. Better death a thousand times over, even a death as hideous as this, than that the girl he loved should agree to this black-souled fiend's demands! But why did his eyes refuse to close, to blot out the impending agony? Why did soul-chilling numbness creep through him now, freezing him in the face of hideous death?

He wanted to scream words of defiance, but could not. The tongue in his mouth was a bloated lump of flesh jammed against his teeth. His lower lip was almost bitten through, and the trickle of hot blood was salt as acid, dribbling into his throat.

A quarter-inch more and that glowing nail-point would sear his eyeball. There would be a moment of blinding pain—then merciful oblivion. And, if he lived, he would never again see sunshine, or people talking, or the face of the girl he loved....

But that crimson point came no nearer. Old Merritt was speaking in mocking tones to the girl at the fireplace.

"It is for you to say, my dear. If you come to me willingly, I grant your lover his sight—and his mind. If you refuse, this lovely red finger of mine will caress his eyes and you will smell flesh burning—and the agony will make a gibbering idiot of him. What is your answer?"

No trace of color remained in the girl's face. White as chalk, she stared at the rigid mask that was the face of the man she loved. A liquid sob shook her body. She looked down at herself, at her nakedness, raised her head slowly and gazed in horror at the corpse-faced fiend who desired her. If she spoke the word that would save her lover's life, those leprous hands would....

"*What is your answer!*"

"Oh God, what must I promise?"

"To be mine. Mine for tonight."

"You—you mean—"

"I mean you must promise to be mine. Mine!"

Stark terror gripped the girl's soul. Her eyes closed, as if to blot out hideous visions that stormed her brain. Bravely she fought for self-control, made her rigid body cease its violent trembling. Her lips parted to whisper her answer.

But Milton Perry spoke first.

"Don't do it! If you love me, don't sell your soul to him. Jan—"

Old Merritt shrugged. The glowing nail moved a fraction of an inch nearer to Perry's gaping eyes. "I am waiting, my dear. And I shall not wait much longer."

"Don't do it, Jan! In the name of God, don't promise—"

"Oh God, I must!" Slowly the girl turned, focused her gaze on old Merritt's leering face. "I—I—"

"*Don't do it, Jan!*"

"I—promise—anything you say," the girl moaned. "Anything—you—ask."

The words came as if wrung from her throat by hands of torture. The fiend's answer was slow in coming, too, and was a mirthless laugh, barely audible. Milton Perry shuddered, moaned dully and went limp in the chair that supported him. Very quietly, old Merritt withdrew the instrument of torment and stepped back.

Outside, storm-wind whined a death dirge of black mockery, and gusts of wind-driven rain rattled against shut windows. No other sound disturbed the suspense-laden silence. But in Milton Perry's soul a voice of despair shrieked in soundless agony, and madness clawed at his mind.

It was over—all over. No matter what happened now, the girl he loved would keep her promise. She had given it; she would keep it. He knew her well enough to know that.

This night, that lovely body would belong to the monstrous creature who stood there in semidarkness, chuckling now in obscene triumph. Those leprous hands....

Slowly, very slowly, old Merritt moved toward his promised victim. The girl cringed from him, stifled a cry of horror. But the bony hands did not reach out. Motionless in the pale glow of the fire, Merritt returned the girl's stare, laughed mockingly.

"There is no hurry, my dear. First, let me show you something."

The gaunt hands reached up, flung aside the sodden felt hat that had so long shaded those rotted features. The thin fingers curled, ripped downward, tearing away decayed flesh. Then, with deliberate lack of haste, the stooped shoulders straightened, slid clear of the shapeless black garment that had covered them.

"And now, my dear, perhaps you will be even *willing* to spend this night with me. Look!"

The fiend drew a deep breath, inflated his sunken chest. Turning, he gazed squarely into the girl's face; and that face filled slowly with amazement. Milton Perry, staring from across the room, went suddenly stiff and gripped the chair-arms with nerveless fingers.

For the creature who stood there in the fireglow—stood there straight and tall, stripped of the sodden black outer garment and drooping felt hat—was no longer the dead-alive specter of Benjamin Merritt. That leering face was no longer a sunken, rotted mask risen from the grave. It was a sallow, smiling face, good looking save for the unholy lust that transformed it. And the man's hands, rubbed clean of the chalklike substance that had whitened them, were lean-fingered and normal.

That gloating, hungry-eyed fiend of hell was Everett Latham!

LATHAM laughed softly.

"You see, my dear," he said, "I planned this very carefully, from the beginning. It was I who gave old Merritt the happy idea of the death-curse and urged him to join Ora Fiske's tribe of fanatics at the courthouse that morning. It was I who invited him into a restaurant, an hour or so before the excitement began, and dropped caffein tablets into his coffee. His heart was already weak, and I hoped that the extra caffein, plus the coming splurge of excitement, would kill him. It did, very effectively—and to my good fortune, in such a way that your lover thought himself guilty of Merritt's dramatic demise."

Mocking laughter spilled from Latham's lips as his hungry eyes drank in the girl's loveliness. "Then, my dear, I built a definite scheme of action and followed it through methodically. I murdered Martin Gregg because he objected to my being taken into the newly-formed manufacturing project. I usurped one of your father's tell-tale shoes, planted it on the hotel fire-escape, and framed him for the killing. And while your worthy father brooded in jail, I went to console him and gave him cigarettes that poisoned him.

"It was necessary, my dear, that I exterminate your family. I have succeeded. Your father is dead; your mother is dying of the shock. You will die before I leave here. And I—as perhaps you may recall—am next in line to inherit a very sizable fortune from your beloved father. There will be the Fiskeville Bank, and the home you have lived in, and—but it is a very worthwhile stake, I assure you. And worth working for."

He shrugged crookedly. "Disguising myself as old Merritt was really very simple. I've studied sculpture, you know. I'm really quite clever with clays and stains, and I knew Merritt intimately enough to ape his mannerisms as well as his appearance."

Slowly Latham turned, peered at Perry. "And you, in your ignorance, made me a prominent member of your new organization, old man." The "old man" had a mocking ring to it. "With you out of the way, I shall find it rather easy to work myself into full control, both of the organization and its funds! You were a fool, Perry, to put so much faith in the power of an old man's curse. You were a further fool to think that I was made deathly ill by my supposed efforts to help you.

"I poisoned you that night. As old Merritt's resurrected corpse, I gave you three days to live. Then I dropped poison into the very coffee you drank twenty minutes later to soothe your nerves. A slow-acting poison, gradually producing sickness and death. Later I succeeded in administering the same dose to your sweetheart."

Perry's bloodless lips formed a snarling answer but abandoned it. Poison? It had been poison, then, not the curse, that had made him so deathly, ill. Perhaps the suicide potion he had spilled into his own throat had acted as an antidote. But Janice—if she, too, were poisoned....

He sat like a propped-up corpse, staring with eyes that refused to close. Even now, the girl he loved might be near to death! She had been ill when she had first fought her way through the storm, seeking him. If she were not taken to a doctor soon....

He groaned aloud at the thought. No doctor would ever again see that lovely body alive. Latham would have no mercy.

"You see," Latham said, "I shall come into my own this night. By morning, the Jordons will be extinct; I shall inherit their money and their possessions. Milton Perry will have vanished, presumably the victim of an old man's curse, and I shall have control of an up-and-coming business enterprise. Also, I shall have obtained a full measure of revenge upon Perry for his cruelty in robbing me of the girl I desire. And while he looks on in torment, I shall possess his loved one for a few hours of indescribable bliss."

He swung about, leered at Perry. "She is beautiful, no? As beautiful as those lovely flowers of yours, before I poured acid on their roots. And when I am finished with her, she too will fade and die—before your eyes."

The smile faded from Latham's lips. Abruptly he stepped toward the near-naked girl who stared at him in horror. "You made a solemn promise. If you break it, I shall continue the torture of your sweetheart where I left off. Are you ready to keep your word?"

The girl made no answer. Her reply lay in the sudden droop of her head. She had given her word: she would keep it no matter how great the agony. It was the reply Milton Perry had expected.

Like a madman, Perry surged forward in the chair that held him. Shrill words spilled from his throat, smothering the pitiful sobbing sounds that ebbed from Janice Jordon's pale lips.

"Damn you, Latham! If you so much as put a hand on her—"

Latham's only reply was a soft laugh, laden with triumph. He took a step forward, reached down and unfastened the chains that encircled the girl's ankles. Without even turning his head to favor Perry with a glance, he freed her arms, stepped back and murmured softly:

"Tonight, my dear, is ours. Yours and mine. Come...."

She stood rigid, staring at him with wide eyes that begged silently for mercy. But no mercy lay in that lustful gaze.

"*Come!*"

SLOWLY, as if weighted to the floor, Janice Jordon moved toward his waiting arms. And in the agony-racked brain of Milton Perry, something snapped.

A lurid oath spewed from his foam-flecked lips as he strained forward. Blind fury gave him the strength of a madman. The chair beneath him cracked with a splintering crash and broke clear of the restraining bar of the couch. With an effort more than human, he wrenched one foot up and out, fraying the rope that held his ankles. The rope broke.

What happened then was the result of blind instinct. Head foremost, he hurtled across the room, shoulders hunched, knees high. The shattered chair still clung to him; his arms were doubled behind him, lashed at the wrists. But he needed no hands. The fury of his charge carried him forward with the force of a battering-ram. His lowered head crashed with bone-breaking impact into the pit of Latham's stomach.

As if bent by giant hands, Latham staggered backward, retching.

The wall stopped him, but he had no time to sidestep the furious onslaught of his assailant. Again Perry's head and shoulders drove home with sickening force, before outstretched hands could form a barrier. Breath shrieked from Latham's lips; his face purpled. He staggered on limp legs, clawed the wall for support as he stumbled sideways.

Perry stood swaying, gathering strength for a final charge. The snarl that quivered his lips was the battle-cry of a jungle killer defending its mate. He lurched forward.

Behind him, Janice Jordon cried shrilly: "Wait! Wait, Milt! He'll kill you!" Cold hands touched the wrists that were bound behind him, worked frantically to loosen the ropes that encircled them. Across the room, Latham was rigid on widespread legs against the wall, and the man's right hand, seemingly half-paralyzed, was fumbling desperately to pull something blunt and heavy from a pocket that refused to untangle.

Perry's wrists jerked free. Still snarling, he hurtled forward. In Latham's trembling hand a revolver jerked up, swung level with the torture-marked chest of its intended victim!

Just once the gun belched, filling the room with a sudden staccato roar that drowned Janice Jordon's terror-scream. The slug made a sobbing sound past Perry's convulsed face. Then his clenched fist pistoned to the mark; his left hand shot up, raked the revolver from limp fingers.

Again and again, as Latham fell, Milton Perry swung the gun with mad fury, until the agonized face of the man before him was a red mask of terror. The gun slid from his fingers then and he swayed erect, looked down without compassion at the shapeless dead thing on the floor.

Then he turned and took a sobbing, near-naked girl in his arms, and whispered: "It's finished, beloved. If what he said is true, there's poison in your system and we need a doctor. But after that, it's—finished."

Janice clung to him closely and did not speak. Outside the house, the wind sang a chant of triumph, and the impact of storm-driven rain, less savage than before, was like the gleeful clapping of a million tiny hands.

THE END

Made in the USA
San Bernardino, CA
28 December 2018